THERE IS NO LIGHT AT THE END OF THE TUNNEL BECAUSE THE TUNNEL IS MADE OF LIGHT

RYAN SPENCER

TBW BOOKS

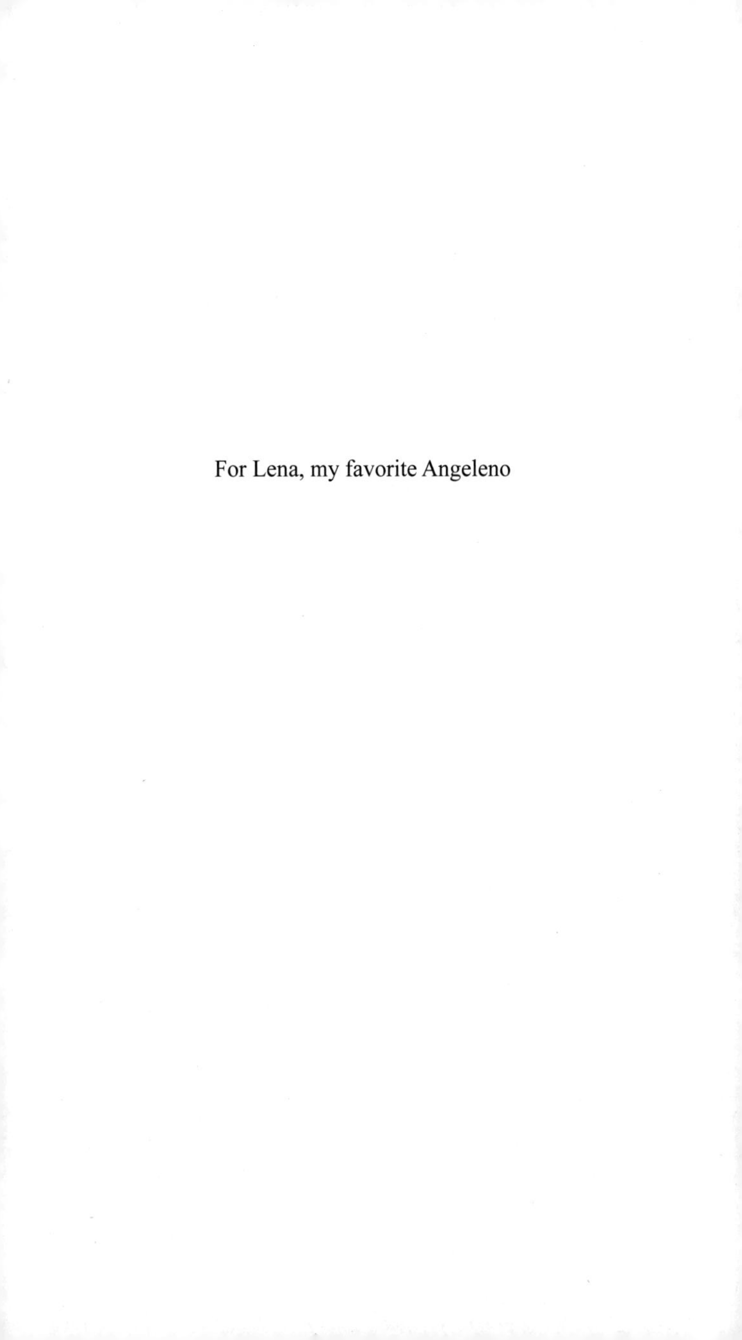

For Lena, my favorite Angeleno

On New Year's Day in Los Angeles

Interviewer: Do you drive Mulholland Drive often?

David Lynch: I live near it, and I drive it quite often. It's a mysterious road. It's rural in many places. It's curvy, it's two lanes, it feels old. It was built long ago, and it hasn't changed too much. And at night, you ride on top of the world. In the daytime you ride on top of the world too, but it's mysterious, and there's a hair of fear because it goes into remote areas. You feel the history of Hollywood in that road.

THIS IS HOW I FIND MYSELF AT THE END OF a pointed gun on the first day of the year in which the forty-fifth president will be sworn into office. On New Year's Day in Los Angeles, my dead car is still in the closed-down shop and the line at the LAX Fox Rent-a-Car is two hours long and the waiting room speakers are belatedly pumping out Top 40 Christmas music. Mariah Carey, Wham!, Paul McCartney, the Pretenders, the Waitresses. Outside the day is already gone. This is my first winter in L.A. and no one has bothered to remind me how dark it gets, how soon.

Sand grits the insides of my shoes. The night before, we burned our intentions, but all the things we tried to leave behind come slithering right back. On the beach this afternoon, the caricatures of the year before, the bros playing touch football, the two girls choreographing their Instagram shoot, assessing the angles and the lip pout, stripping to bikinis in the cold, popping a bottle of champagne inside the hollow of a cove but not even really drinking it. A semicircle of beach witches held a ceremony and nearby, a couple voraciously made out while a kid, with them but apart, huddled in a hoodie, grimacing in lonely rebellion. In no time, the Instagram girls were discovered by two older men in sunglasses and loose-fitting leather pants who introduced themselves as "Hollywood producers." We didn't need to stick around for the end of this movie. We gathered up our things, said our goodbyes at the top of the cliff, and one of them gave me a lift to Fox.

I have a stupid fondness for Fox Rent-a-Car because it is cheap, because its name has an odd retro zing of place names that exist in a time of the past—Chock Full o'Nuts, the Automat—and because of the clientele it attracts, people who also primarily exist in those liminal worlds. They arrive from towns outside Omaha; they come from Ohio, Oklahoma, Orlando, Spartanburg, and St. Louis, with brown cardboard suitcases inherited from their last family members who ever made it out of state, packed with just a few possessions, their tired eyes waiting to be struck by stars. They will buy maps of the stars' homes. They will go on the Universal Studios tour and they will walk the Hollywood Walk of Fame and they will take a picture on Rodeo Drive and they will pronounce it *ROH-deo*, and they will make faraway photos of the Hollywood sign.

The sound of their accents is friendly to me. I too hail from a place not unlike theirs, dreamed of a place like this. My idea of L.A. was polished by reruns of *The Beverly Hillbillies*, formed by the grainy gossip of the grocery tabloids delivered to our mailbox. I knew what tragedies could befall the rich and famous, the drownings and the divorces and the diets and the drugs. From an early age I also believed I was in tune with L.A.'s dark side.

In the Fox Rent-a-Car parking lot on New Year's Eve my

radio is set to some California AM, something Twilight Zone–esque and wordless, whose hysteric melodies are broken briefly by tolling bells when I drive over the tire spikes and flash my paperwork to the woman in the booth, listening to what I imagine is the same station. She slides back the contract along with a map of the stars, wrinkled and clearly used, with asterisks marked in purple and green ballpoint pen.

Without thinking much about where I am going, I head north. I want the illusion of driving into the night. *There's some dark metallic something razoring around in my chest* is a line that pops into my head. Mary Robison writing in the guise of a character named Money. Money is a screen-writer, a woman who is in the habit of mailing letters to Sean Penn signed "Mrs. Sean Penn." What Money and I have in common is that neither of us has any true business being in L.A., neither of us is married to Sean Penn, and both of us have a habit of aimless, insomniac driving.

Cars thin out on the 405, Los Angeles eerie quiet. Around the fire last night we all played the impossible game of fathoming its significance. How to tell its story. We mea-sured its losses, its staggering election of hate. *The year the music died*, someone said, that someone being me.

There had been an astrophysicist at the party, or at least an astrophysics student—a guy in a plaid flannel shirt on a third date, head shaking *no* as the rest of us went around. The biggest news story of the year? he question-marked. Pointed to the sky: cloudy, waxing crescent moon. Primor-dial black holes, he said. He wasn't even all that stoned. The discovery of a galaxy that is almost entirely made up of dark matter. A galaxy so diffuse we can practically see through it. He key-popped the top off a murky, fizzing beer. You know? The one they call Dragonfly 44. Three hundred light years away. They used a telescope made of camera parts to find it.

Put it another way, he said. Finding Dragonfly 44 suggests that the universe is also made up of other mystery dark matter, still-unknown-to-us particles. Deceptive, fluffy-looking, wispy-looking motherfuckers. They come from a super-dense, super-violent region of space.

Violent? Someone asked. An intergalactic war zone, the scientist answered. Dark matter worn like a bulletproof vest, like a shield. And we stood there stupidly huddled around a cheap hibachi flame as a jacuzzi burped and bubbled nearby. Darkness beyond darkness, he repeated.

Later, when we walked to the top of Mount Washington, a fogged sky pulled up like a rug, covering all the stars. All that was available to us was the future, dark and uncertain.

•••

ON NEW YEAR'S DAY IN LOS ANGELES THE roads are open and empty and the sky is clear and I am staying in a strange place, in a strange part of town. To go to sleep means the year will have really begun. My phone is wide awake, listening.

I want to see plain old everyday stars in the sky, I tell it. I repeat it slowly and searchingly, *plain old every-day sta-aaaaars,* so that the phone can understand. But the phone insists this is not possible. The phone informs me that because of the holiday, Griffith Observatory is closed. And so I turn up the radio, scrolling through the stations, in order to think. Later it will occur to me: Whose idea was it to call New Year's Day a holiday, anyway?

Later in the year, many months later, when I think back to the conversation I hear next on the radio, which itself turns out to be a rebroadcast of a conversation, an interview taped the day after Election Day 2016, I will know one of its speakers as a man who is punched by a protester on the streets of Washington, DC, on Inauguration Day 2017. I will be reminded again of this person in August when he leads a hate parade lit by cheap tiki torches through the streets of Charlottesville, Virginia. But on New Year's Day in Los Angeles, I simply recognize him as a semi-famous white supremacist, a man who has been filmed sieg-heiling his "colleagues." I simply know him as a disembodied voice haunting me as I drive through the Hollywood Hills, wishing I was light years away.

"I'll be honest with you," Richard Spencer is saying as I exit the freeway. "Fairness has never been really a great value in my mind. I like greatness and winning and dominance and beauty. Those are values. Not really fairness."

He is being interviewed by Al Letson, the African American host of the show *Reveal*. "So [static-static] is your perfect candidate," Letson says. I can feel the temperature drop as I climb. The distance stretching between streetlights, the sky dimming. "But what's the difference between you and the racists that like, you know, hung people up from trees? What's the difference between you and the Klansmen who burned crosses on people's lawns? What's the difference between you and, you know, the people who don't look at me, an African American man, as a full human being?"

"I don't, you know, look, I'm not going to comment about you know some hypothetical Klansman or whomever,"

Spencer says. I used to think that driving through a cold pocket meant there were woods close by. Now I just think: dark matter.

On the radio they carry on, calm and civil, clear thin ice on the verge of shattering. "There's no such thing as a hypothetical Klansman because the people that I'm talking about exist," Letson says. "They have lynched people. They've done horrible, horrible things. They are the first American terrorists. So it's not hypothetical. I'm not comparing you to this thing that I'm just dreaming up. I'm comparing you to history. And I'm not intrigued by your ideas. I'm saying to you that, like, your ideas sound just like them, except you wear a nice suit and you can speak to me directly. And I respect that about you. I respect that you and I can have this conversation, that you're not wearing a hood, but it's the same thing. And so that's what I'm asking. Like, what is the difference?"

If I squint very hard, I think, I can turn those shadows I see in the median into actual people. Or perhaps just memories, like these two men fizzling into static, their conversation lodged in some lost corner of the universe, somewhere between 2016 and this.

•••

THE PHONE GUIDES ME HIGHER INTO THE HILLS, past still, quiet yards where multicolored Christmas lights glow in the outdoor trees, and eventually up Mulholland Drive. If I can't get to the observatory, take me to the spaceship, I tell the phone, meaning the Chemosphere, John Lautner's 1960s-era flying-saucer-shaped house on stilts, that retro-futurist structure of Brian De Palma's

BECAUSE

Body Double. Inside, I've read, it's destroyed from years of parties. I imagine it sunken and a little hungover and hard to see. But the phone insists on a destination.

In 800 feet, turn left onto Torreyson Drive. I crest a little peak topped by ragged wildbrush, stare into a valley quadrangled into roofs and somber swimming pools. *In 600 feet, in 800 feet...* My compass zigzags, the screen map flies into a recalculating panic, confused by the deep swerves of Mulholland, and my Fox Rent-a-Car radio frazzles into sudden static.

In the dark, trees become curtains. *Turn right.* I swing sharp, toward the dead end of a road that stutters and dead ends at a gaping woods. Roaming grounds of the last mountain lions and coyotes. A lone stammering streetlight. A couple of driveways. I slow down, peer at a mailbox number, several digits wrong. I idle, refresh. My phone map zigzags again and I realize I'm on Torreyson Place, not Torreyson Drive. "What kinda sick individual names a street Edgewood Way—and then put it half a mile away from Edgewood Lane?" says Chris in the first scene of *Get Out*, eight months away in the future of the new year.

The phone stops answering my questions. The phone doesn't tell me not to nose the hood of the Fox Rent-a-Car Toyota into a stranger's driveway to turn around. Siri doesn't tell me to lift my gaze up into the trees. To feel more than just eyes, but feel those too, a twin unblinking, locked on mine. Two glassy little orbs hovering over a barrel of a gun, aimed directly at me. *Freeze*, they say in movies, and I do. With his free pinky finger he draws a wide turn in the air, the trees swarming in black clusters behind him. The fluorescent blast of headlight shines on his chest and his security uniform. With one palm still

THE TUNNEL

raised, I shift, reverse, back out in a single clean slice.

At the mouth of the cul-de-sac the compass zigzags again. In the crackling silence I think for a minute I can actually feel my blood resettling into its veins. I roll down the window and let in the cold, just to breathe. *Turn right*, the phone pipes up energetically over the radio static and who else is there to listen to, honestly? The car obeys, bending down Mulholland; *turn left*, it barks, sending me to the overlook straddling the edge of the Santa Monica Mountains, the canopy of bright false stars of Universal City blotting out the ones overhead.

When a car pulls in beside me, I know who it will be. He flashes his lights twice, slowly, and opens the door of a black SUV, rifle on the front seat I guess, handgun holstered to his belt, his hands raised. Slowly, slowly I raise mine to match.

You all right? the guard says. I didn't mean to scare you. Crazy people. Bad people. Come up here all the time. Now I watch out for him.

I wasn't after anybody, I say. I was lost. (I want to say, how come you don't think I'm one of the crazy bad ones? But I know the answer.)

People come up after him all the time.

After who? I say.

You know, he says. I can't *say* the name. He nods at my rent-a-car paperwork, the map poking out underneath, with its purple and green asterisks. Used to be this was a whole ranch. A farm, they called it. Errol Flynn lived here. You know that? Then Ricky Nelson, then Helen Hunt. By then they'd split the whole property into pieces. Now it's just him. You really don't know?

I shake my head no.

Look, he says. I gotta get back. I was just making sure. Happy New Year, okay? I make my still-raised hand turn into a dull little wave. His gun holster jostles as he walks back to his SUV.

Down the road, sailboats are dry-docked in driveways, houses protruding from the hillsides, built right inside hairpin turns, windows trained on Universal City. I wonder what it feels like to wake and dream on this view, a skyline of failures and successes. *I'd thought he was an actor who had a series canceled*, Eve Babitz wrote of a cowboy she slept with at the Chateau Marmont during the Watts Riots. *He had eyes of canceled blue.*

I can't see Watts from here, not even the towers that came before and outlasted them. I can't see South Los Angeles, where smoke rose in the wake of the LAPD beating of Rodney King, but north and west of lights blotting the stars is the darkness where a neighbor filmed it. I was a teenager across the country, still dreaming of a place like this, when it came on TV. I toss the map of the stars out the window. Like, what's the difference.

There is a loud crack like a shot, or maybe, I want to think, like a branch snapping off a trunk, or a leftover firecracker; there is an echo in the brush below, and then nothing. Were I just a little closer I could smell its smoke. On New Year's Day in Los Angeles, there is a darkness, and a darkness beyond that one, and I drive into them.

...

CRIME SCENE PART ONE

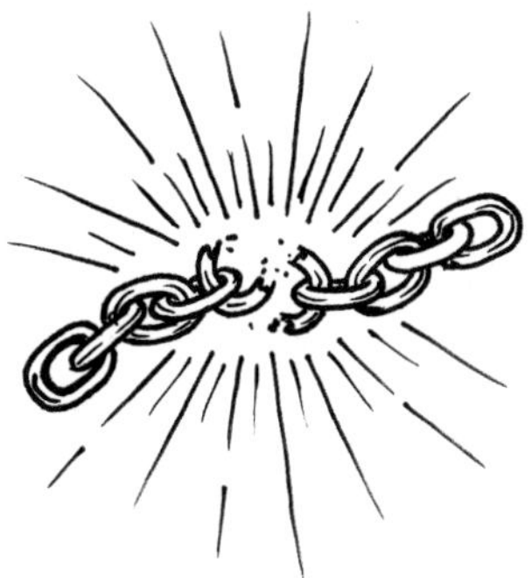

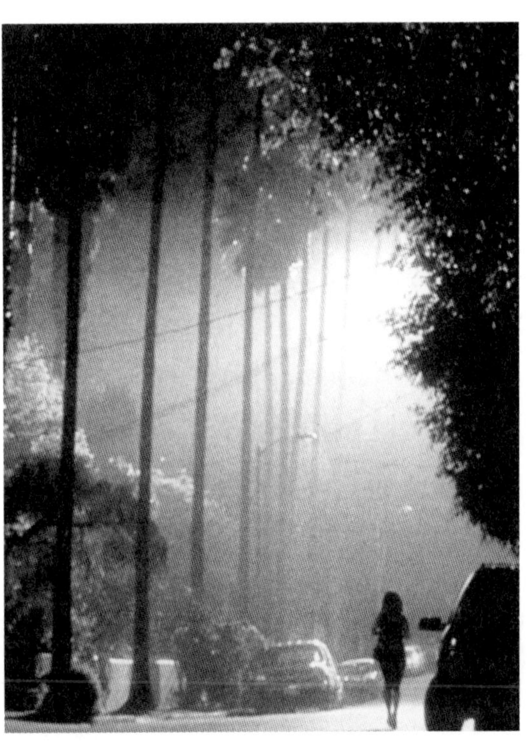

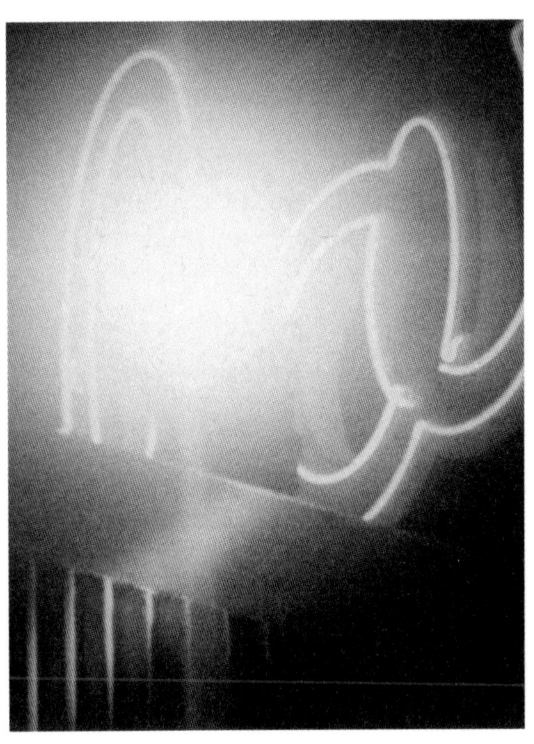

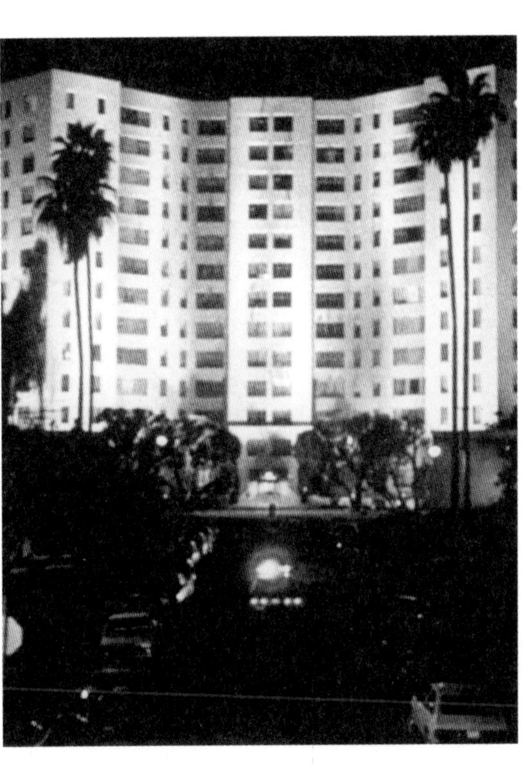

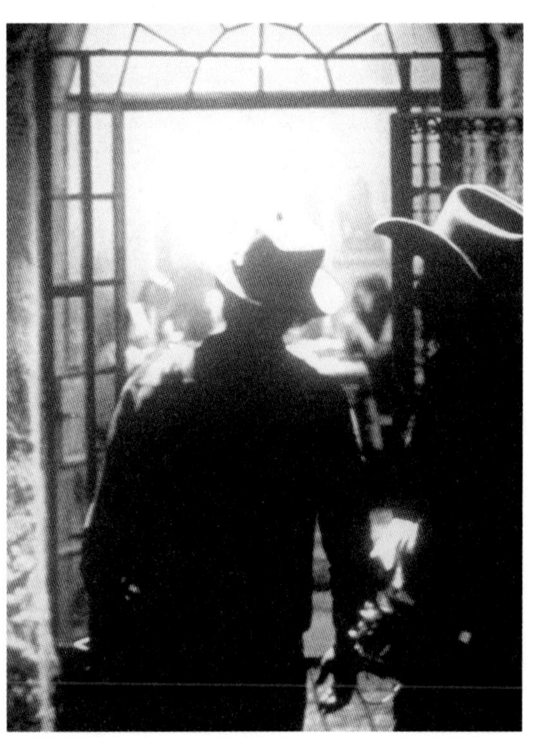

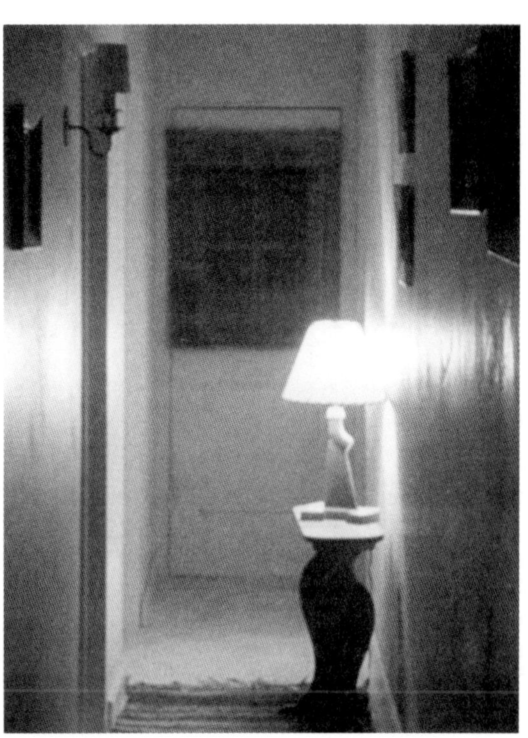

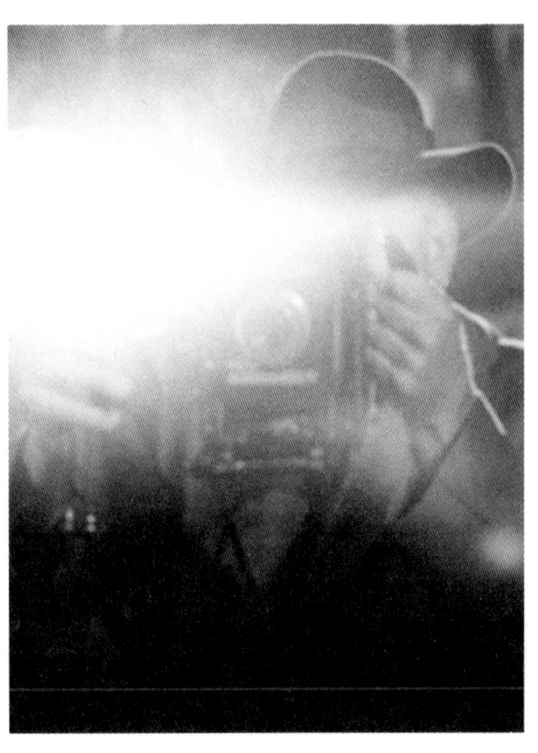

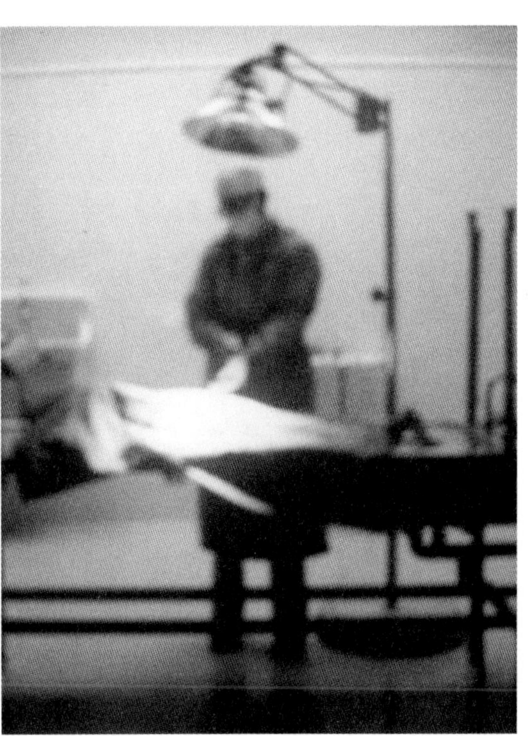

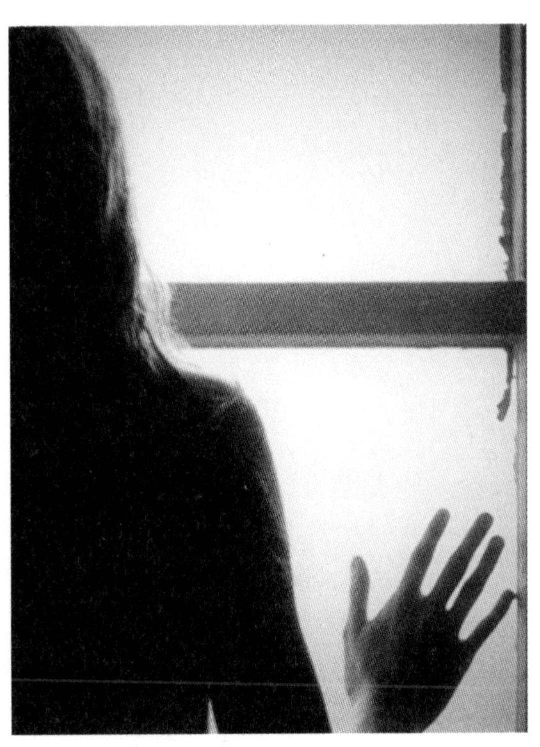

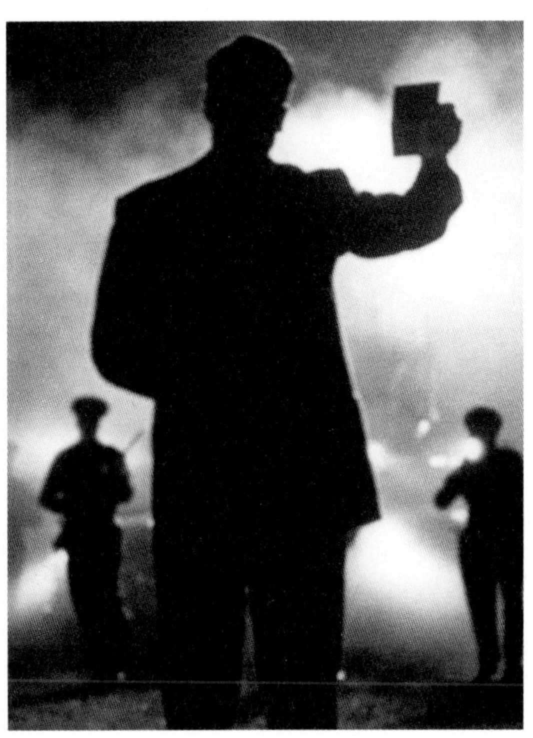

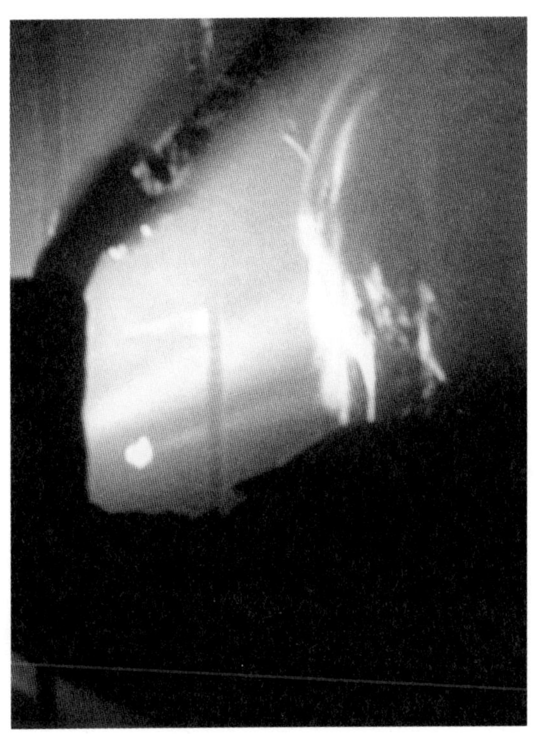

MY ENEMY

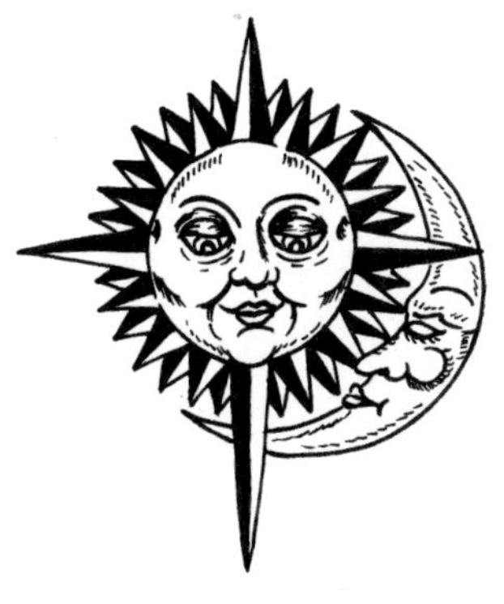

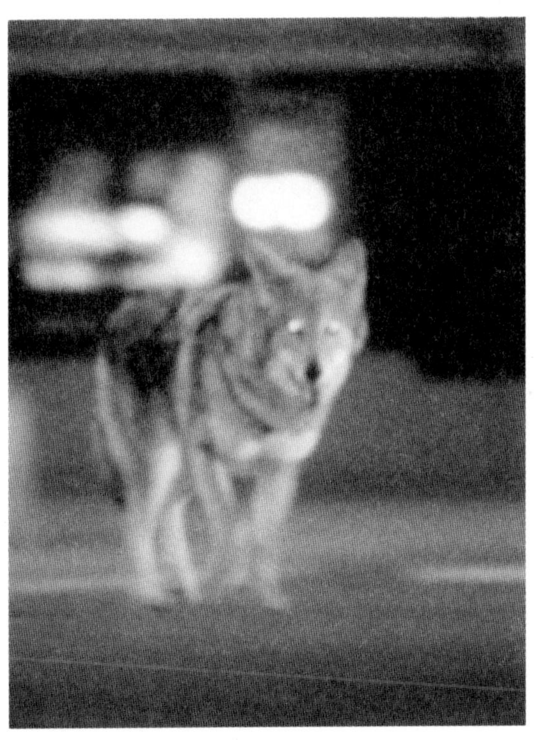

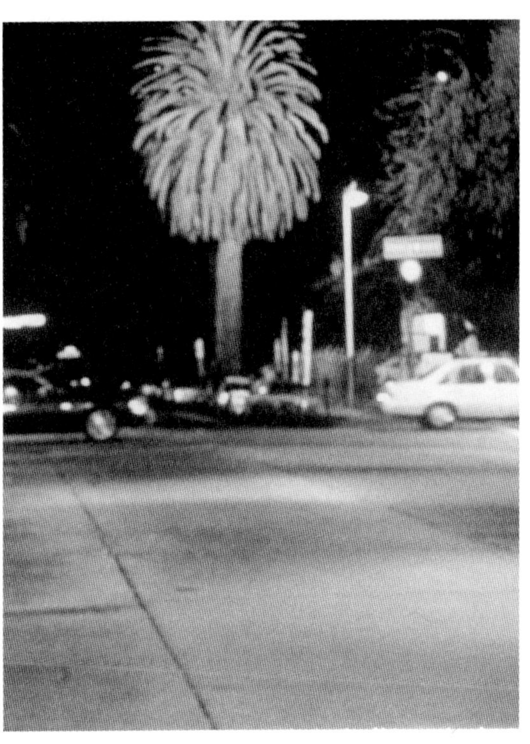

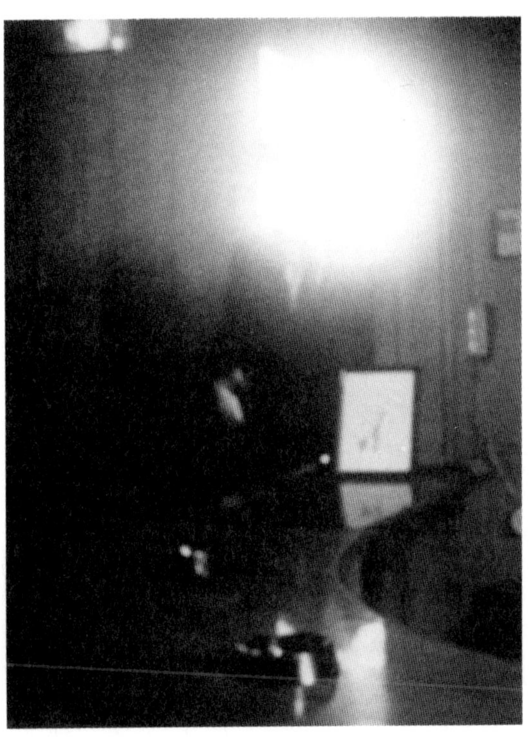

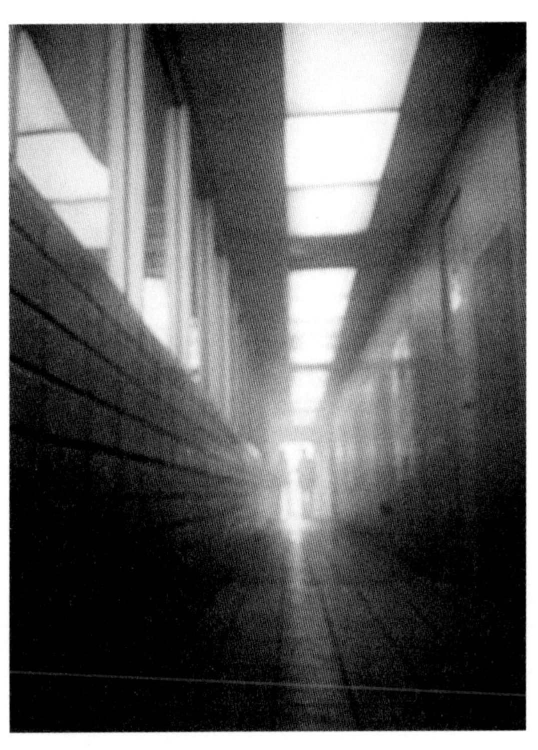

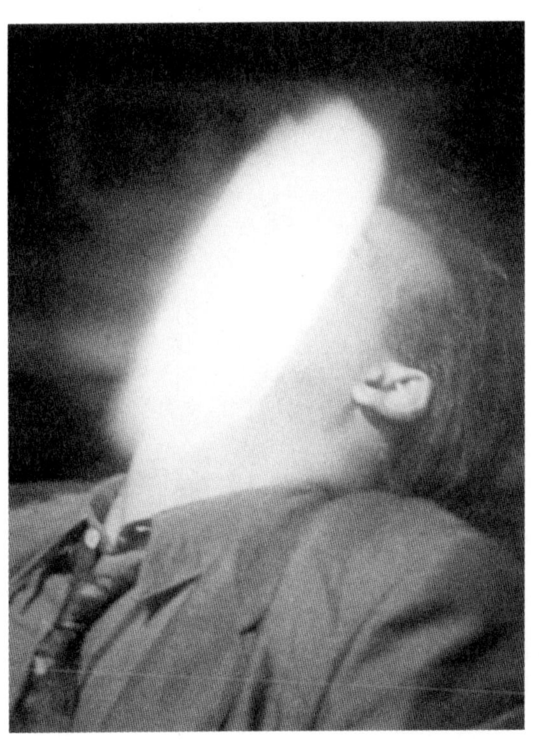

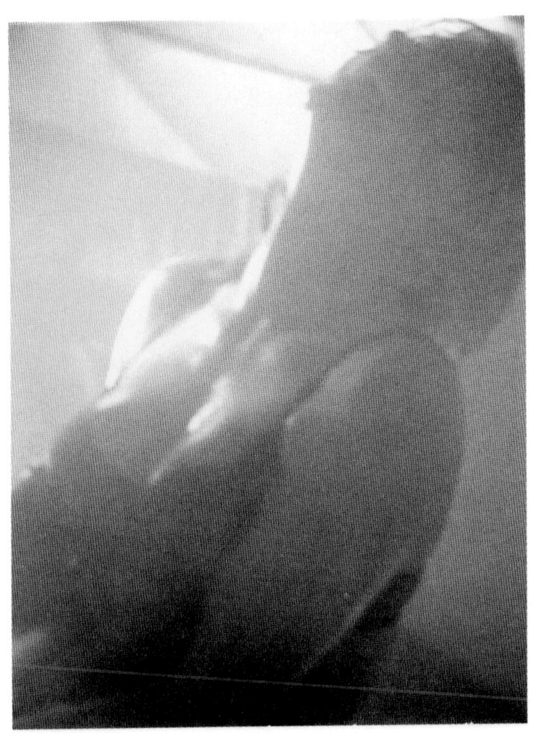

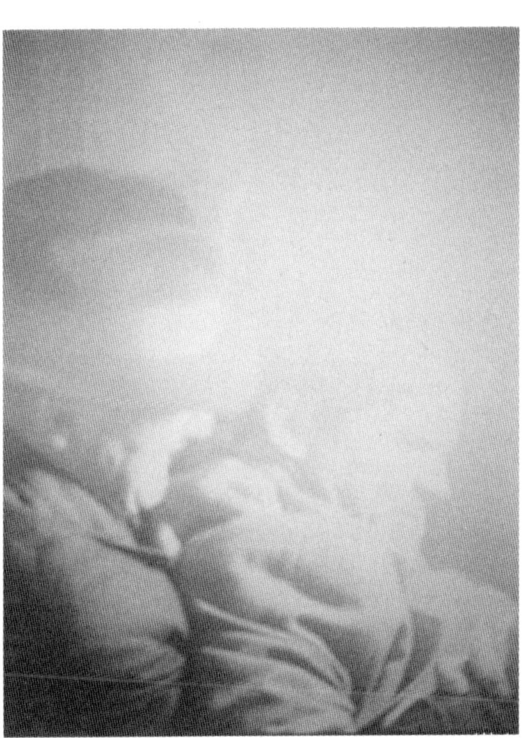

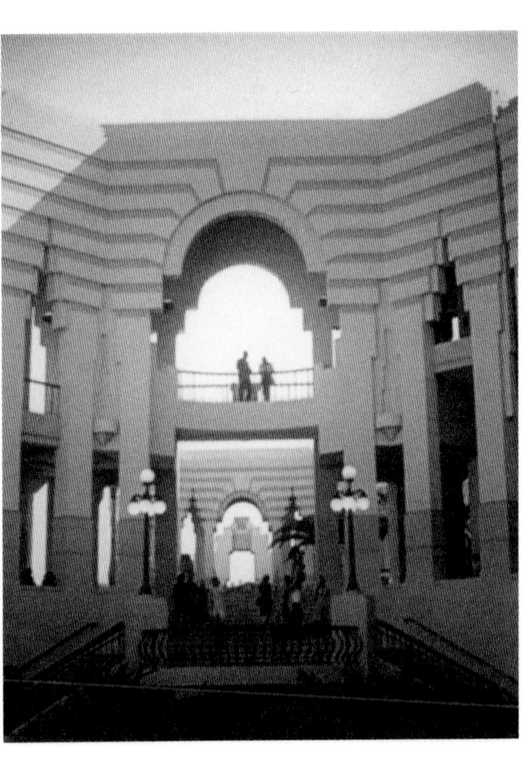

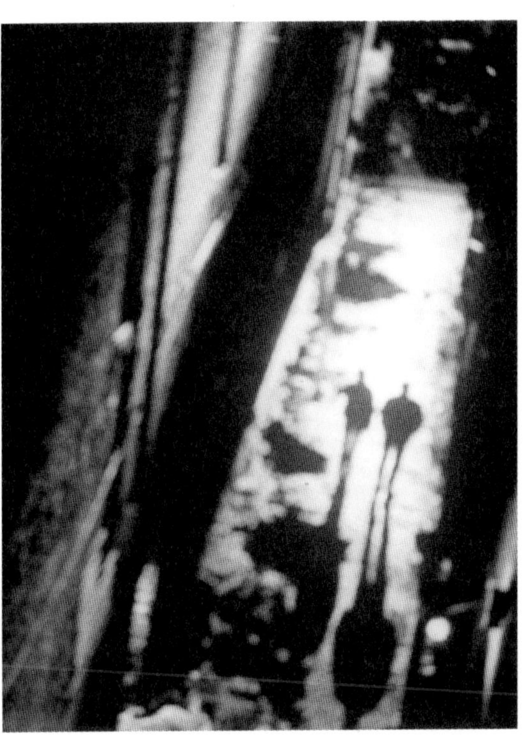

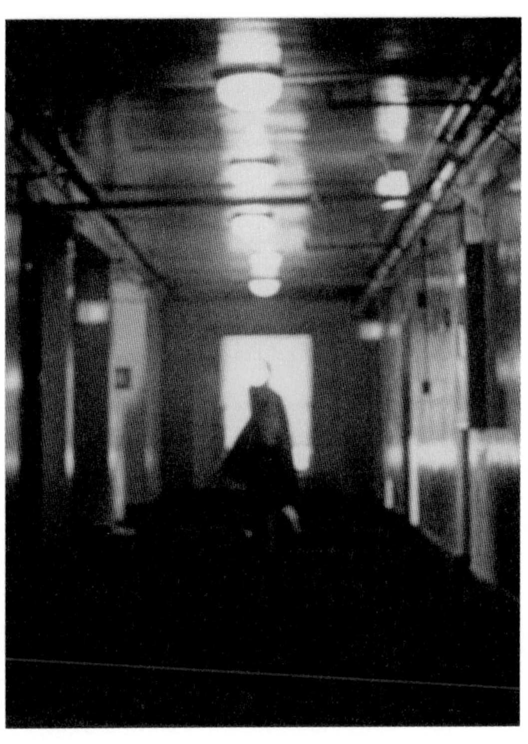

DOUBLE DAY

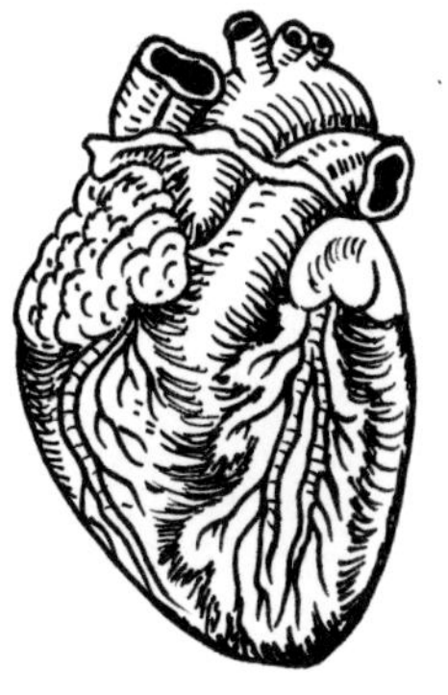

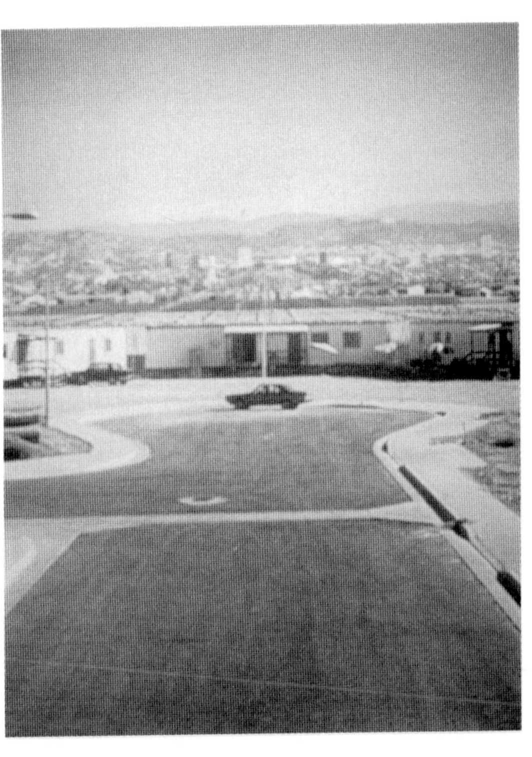

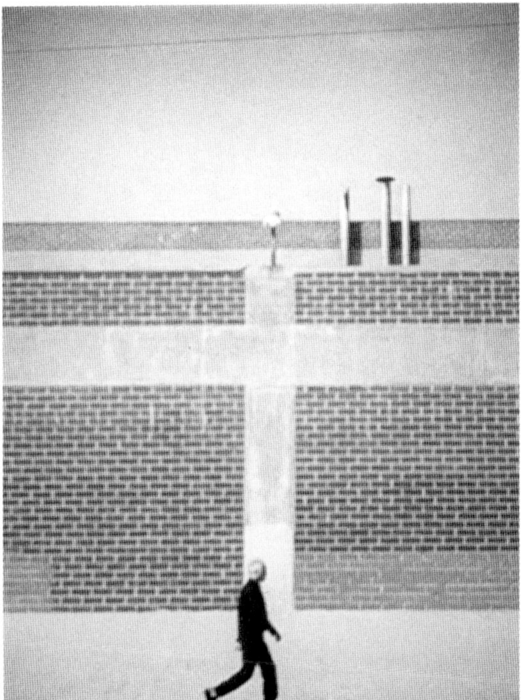

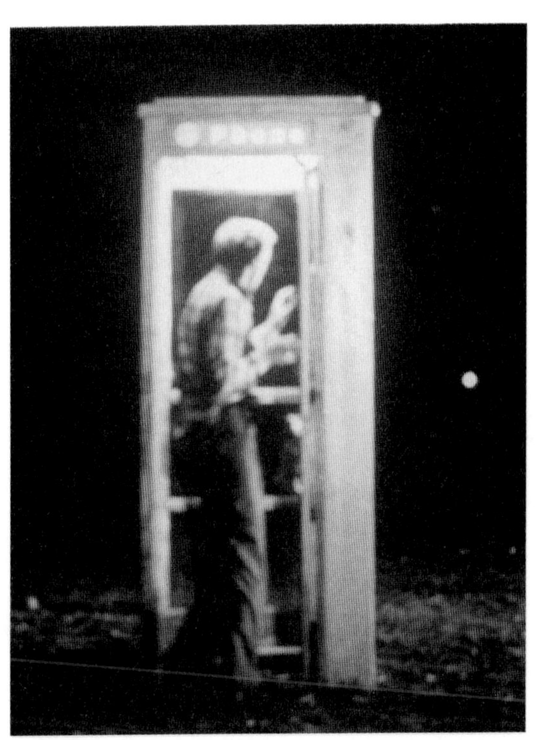

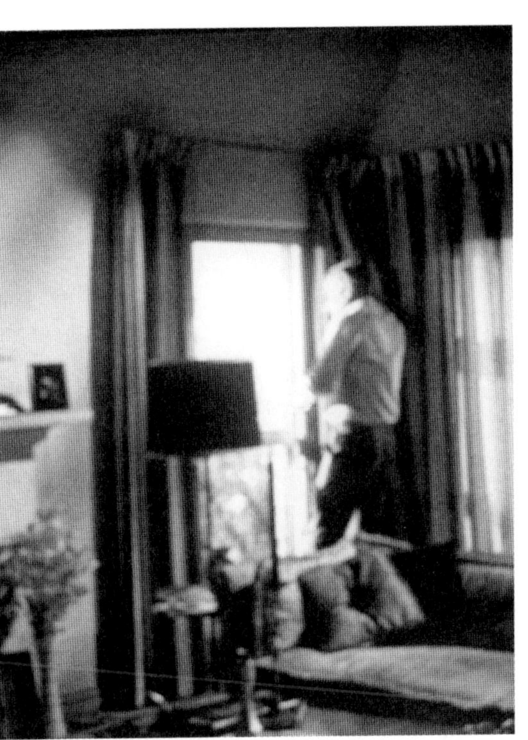

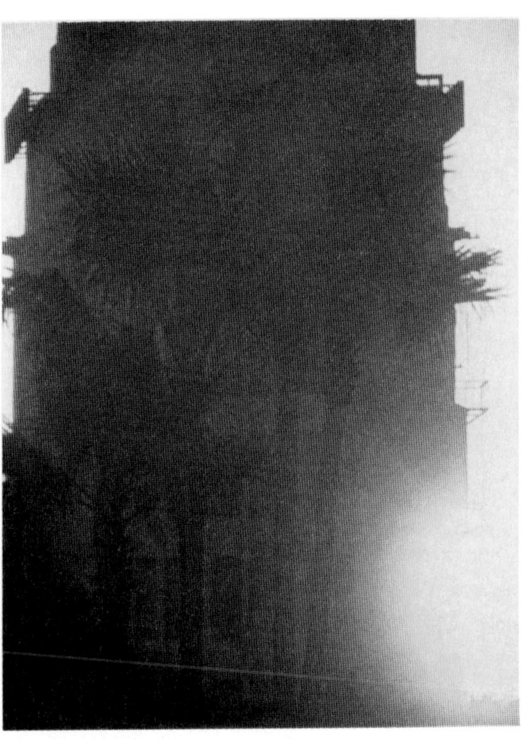

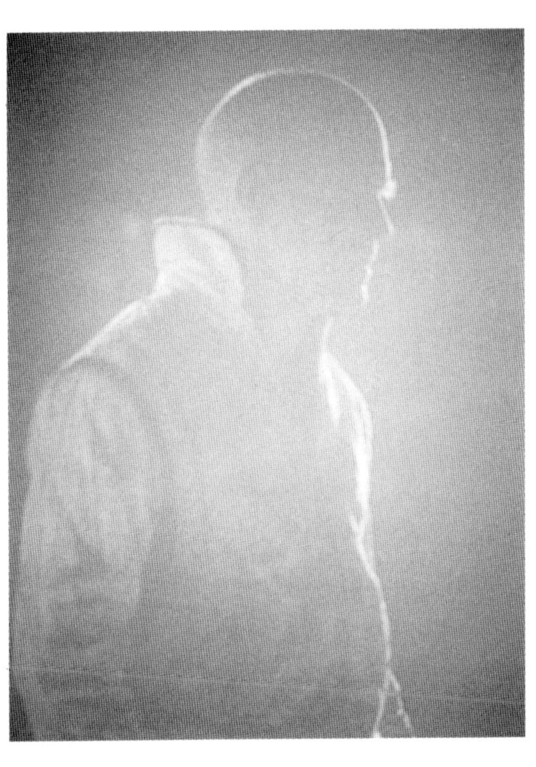

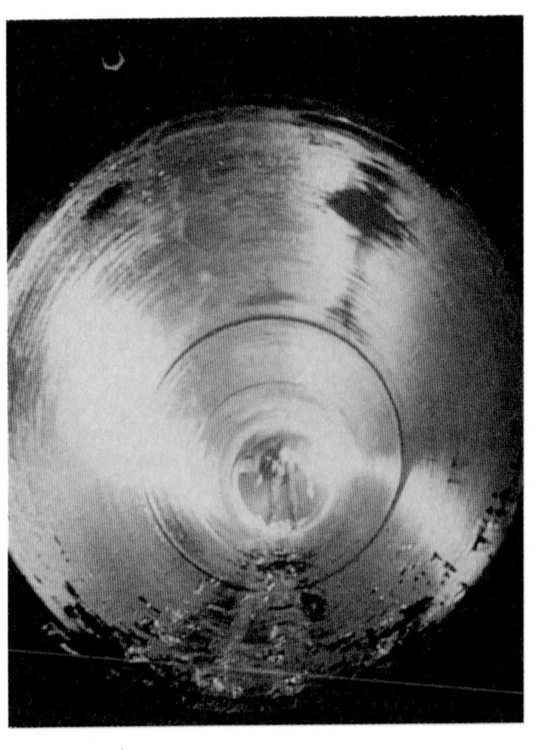

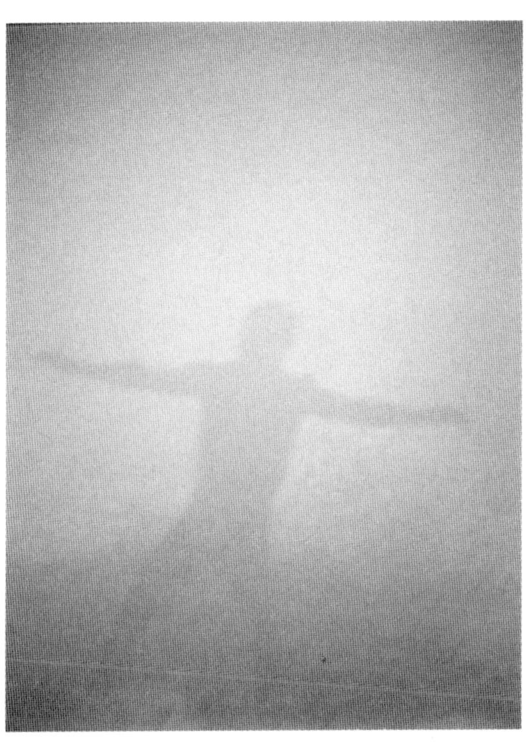

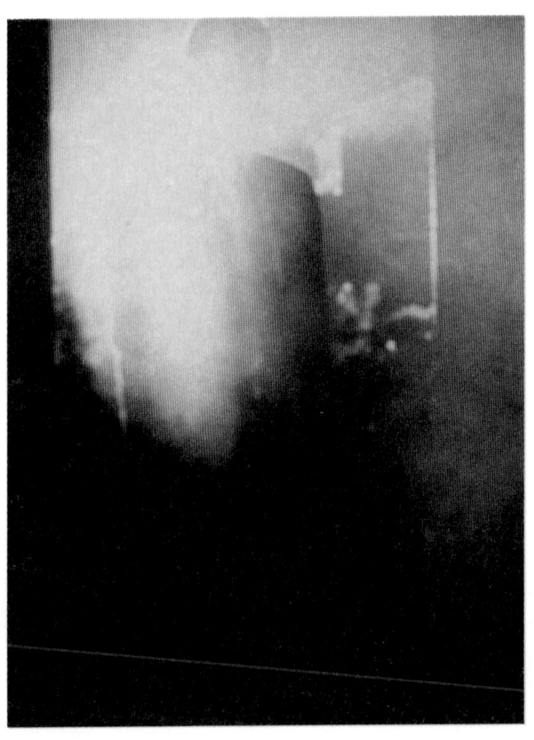

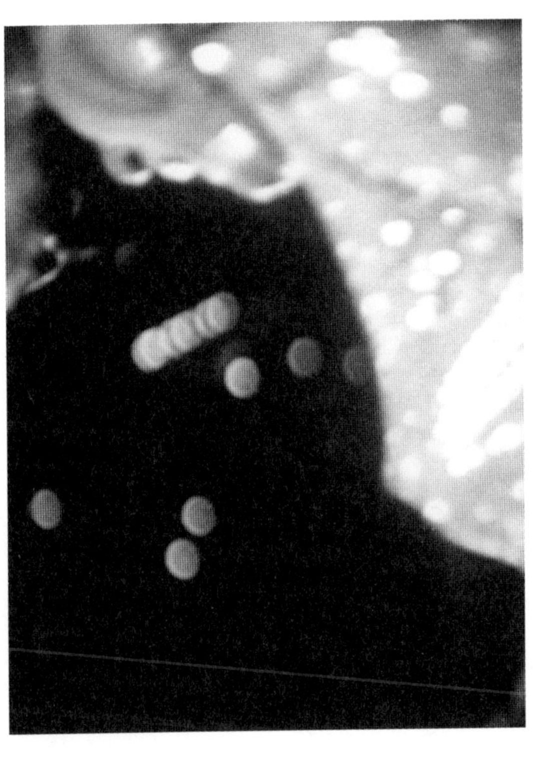

BLAME, ETC.

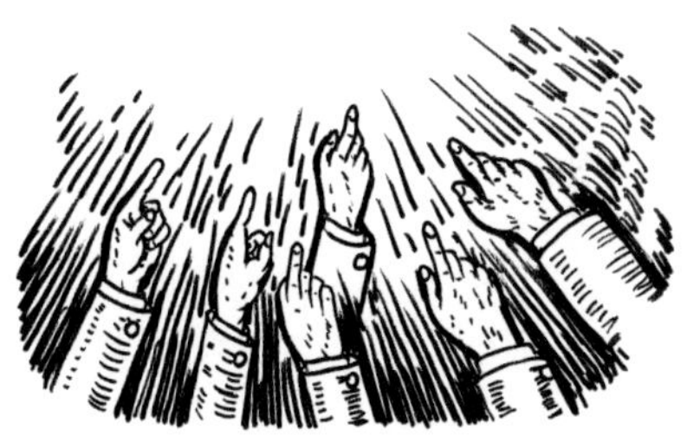

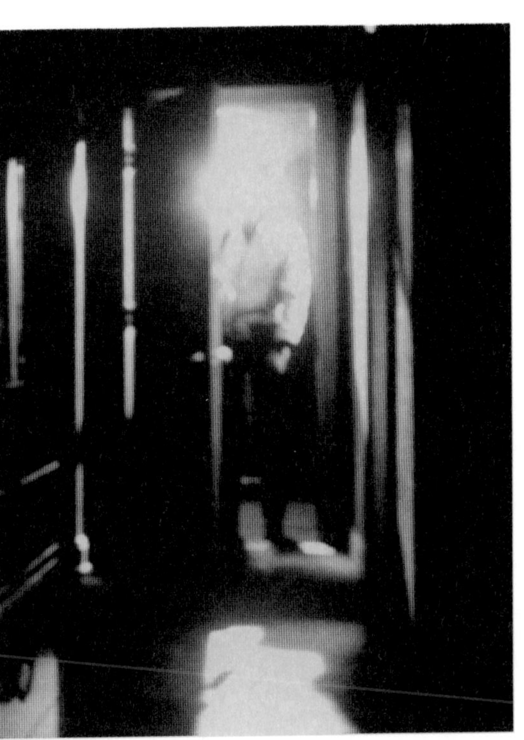

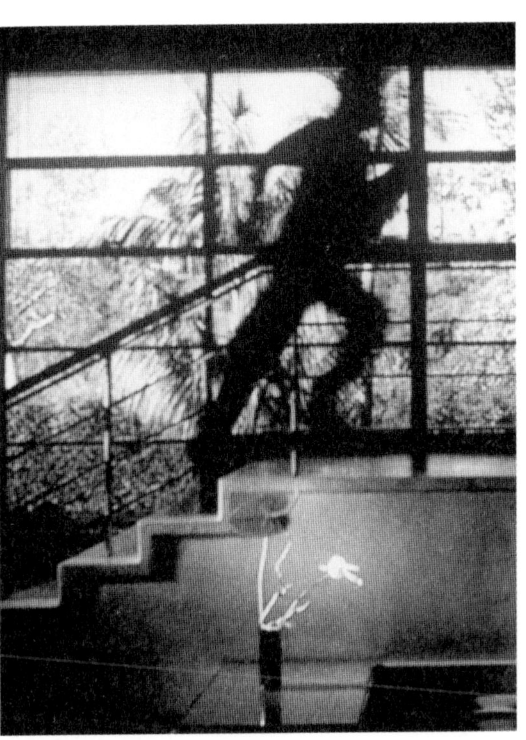

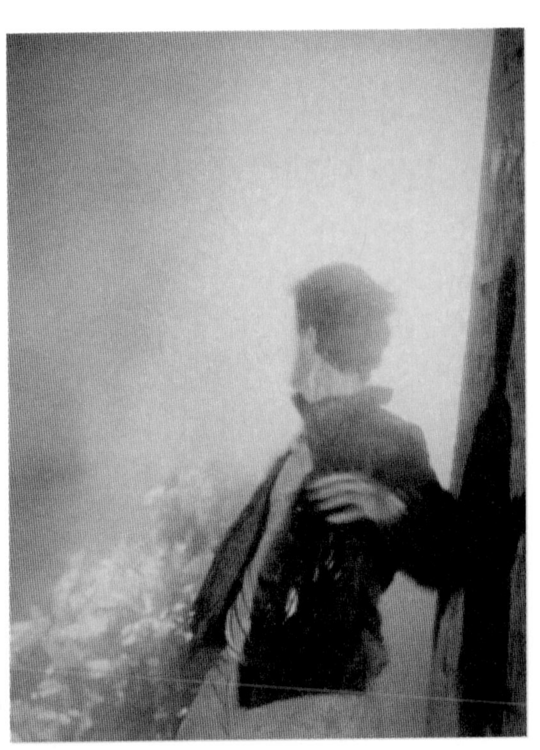

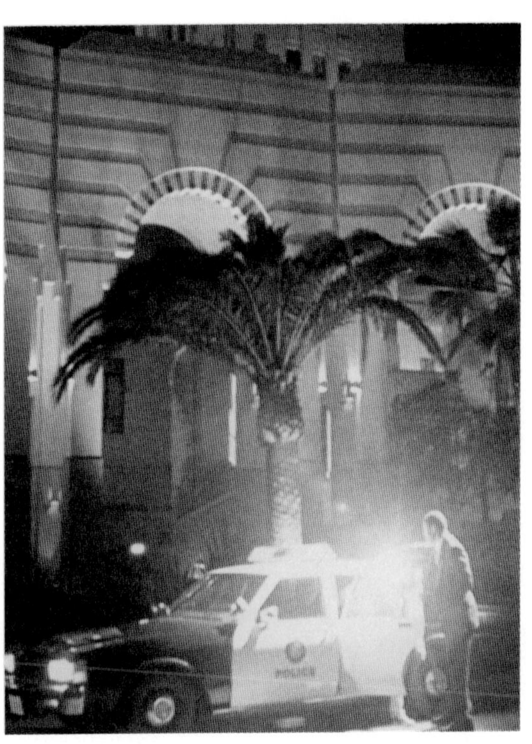

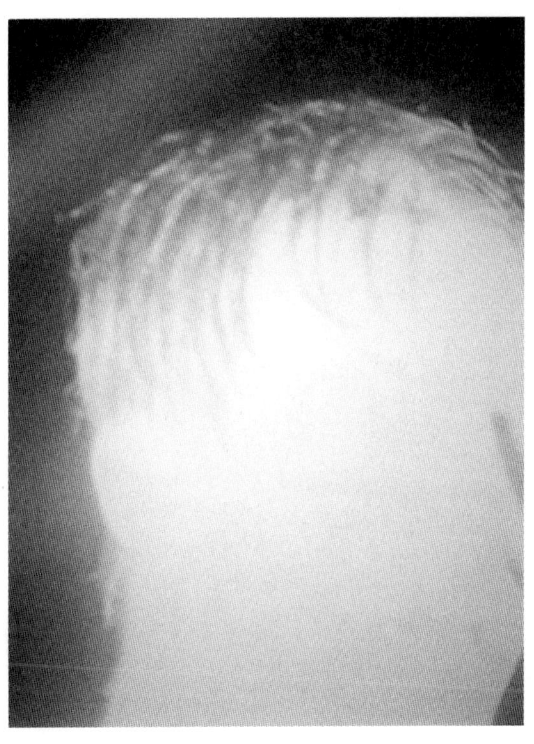

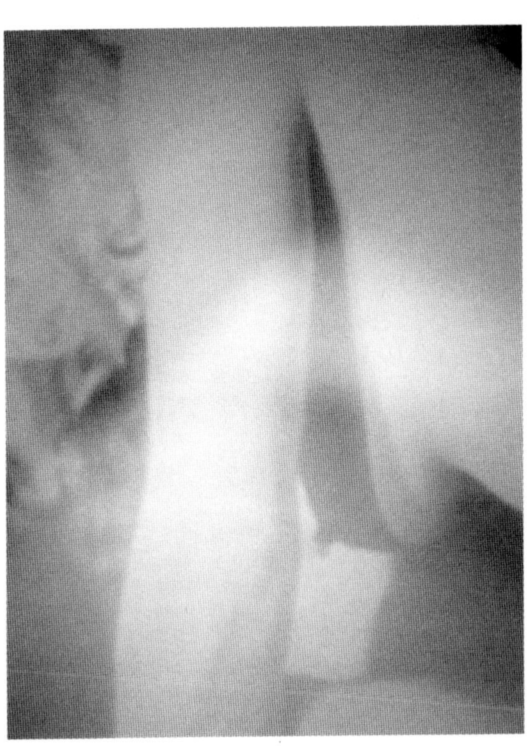

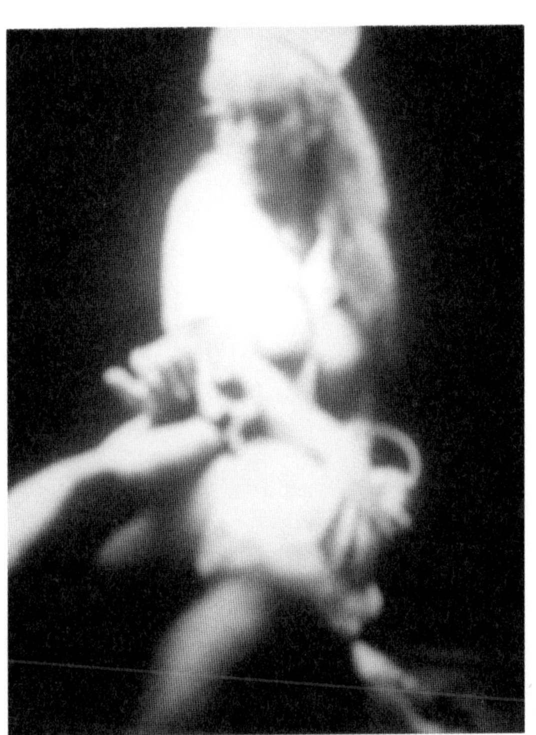

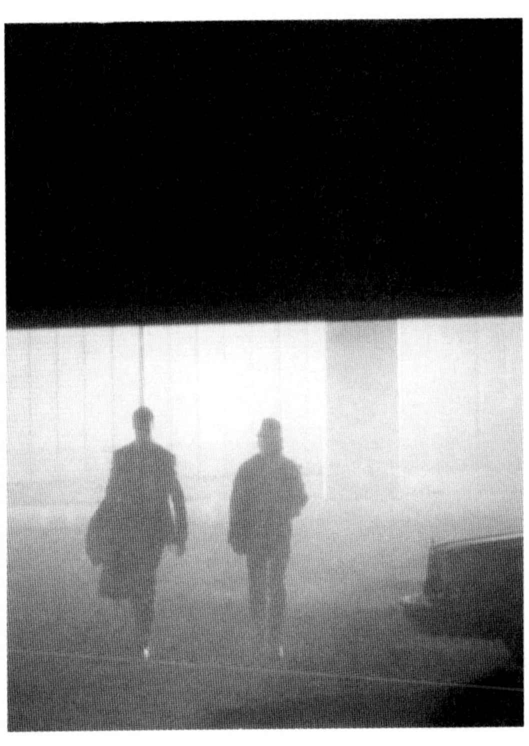

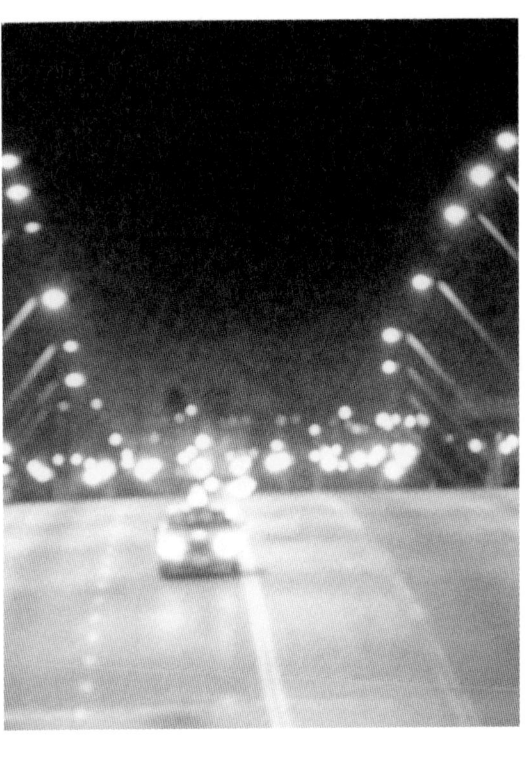

STEP INTO THE LIGHT

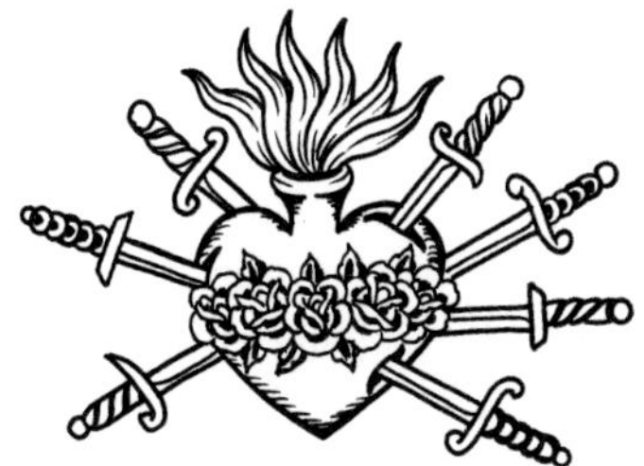

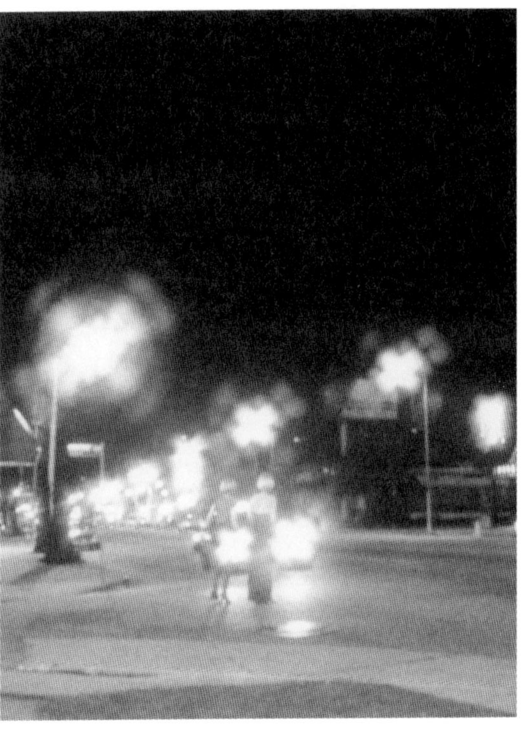

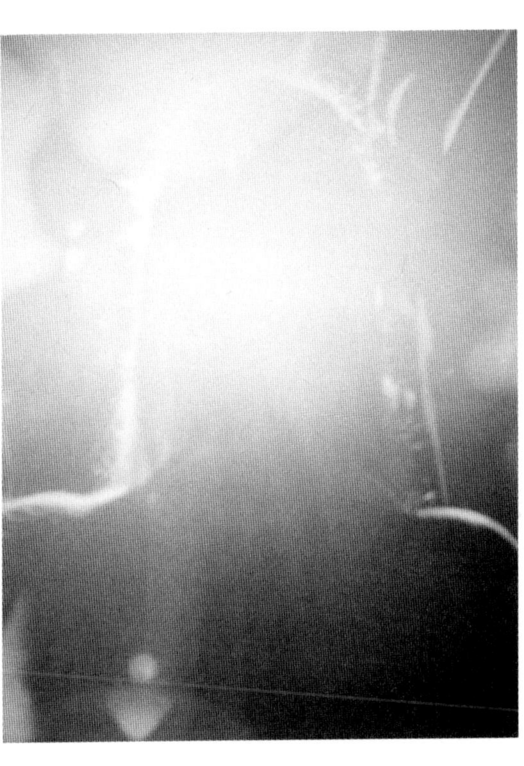

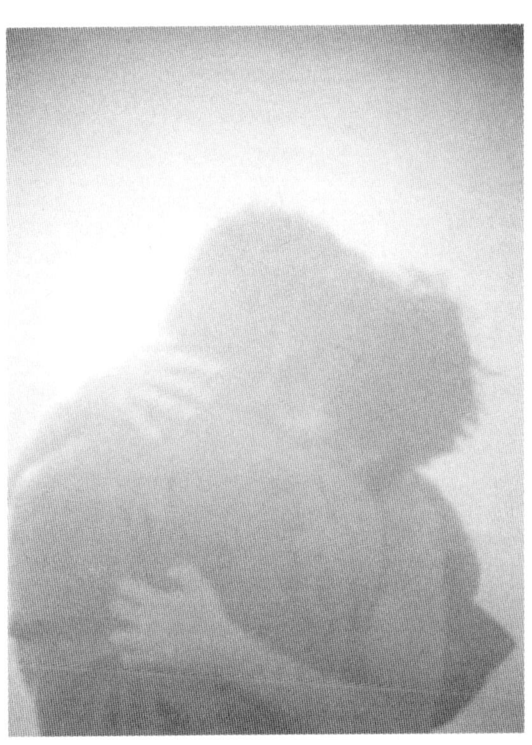

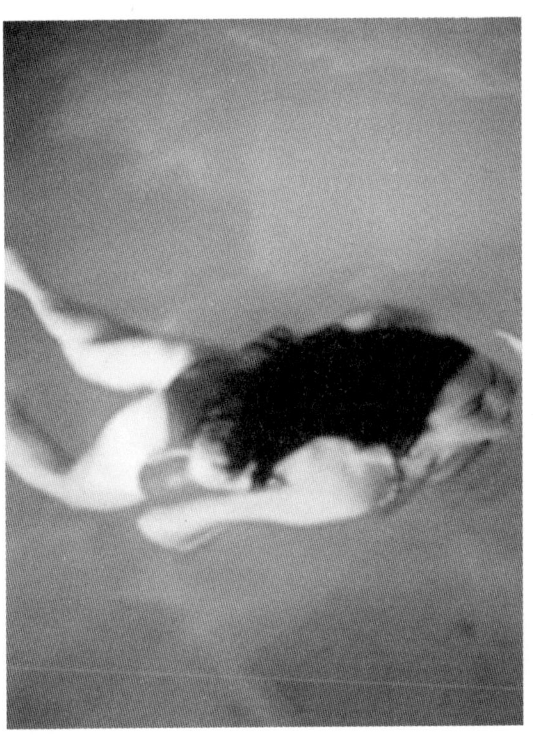

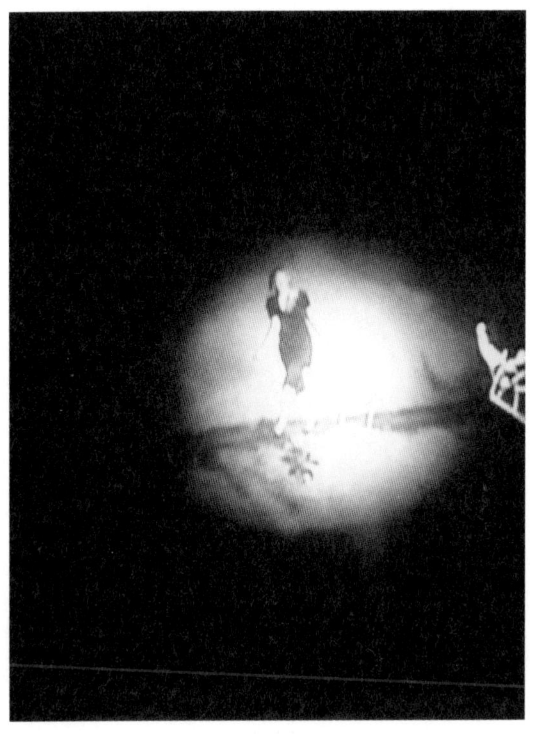

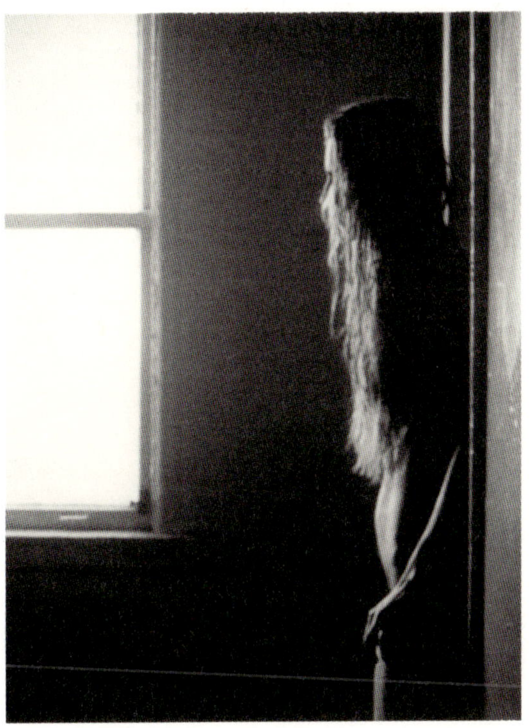

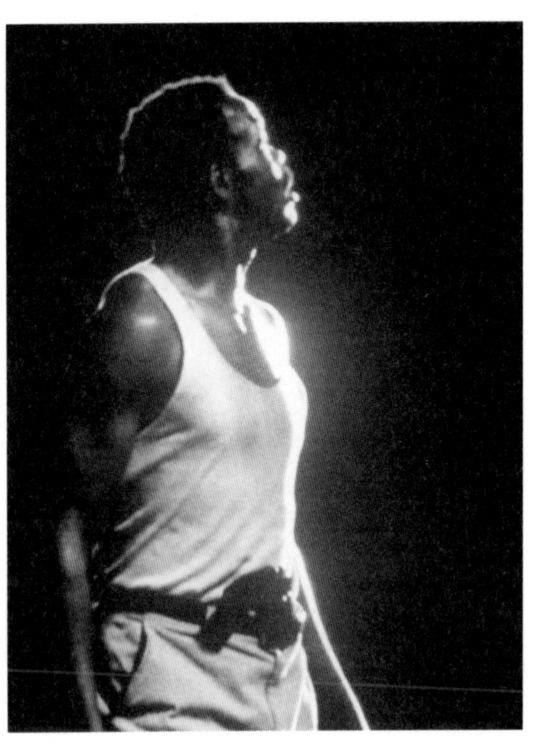

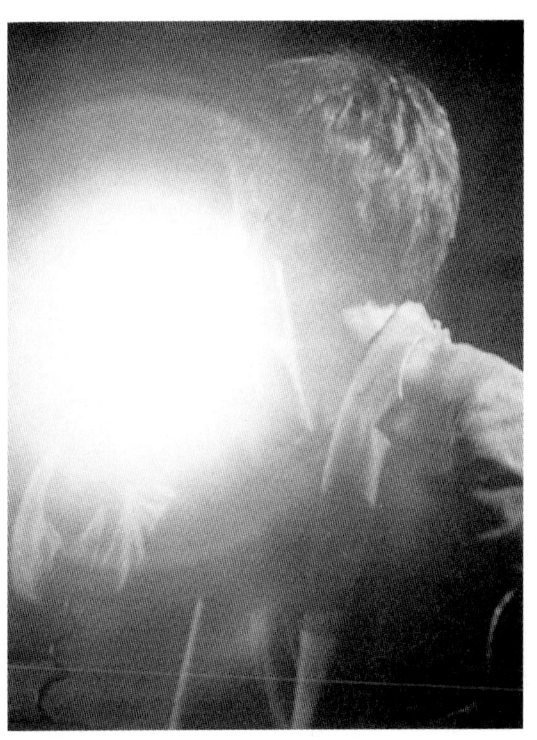

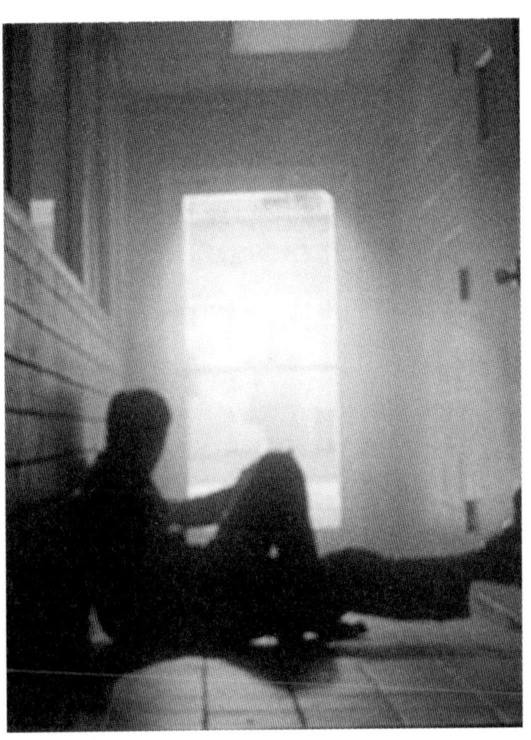

GOING TO TOWN

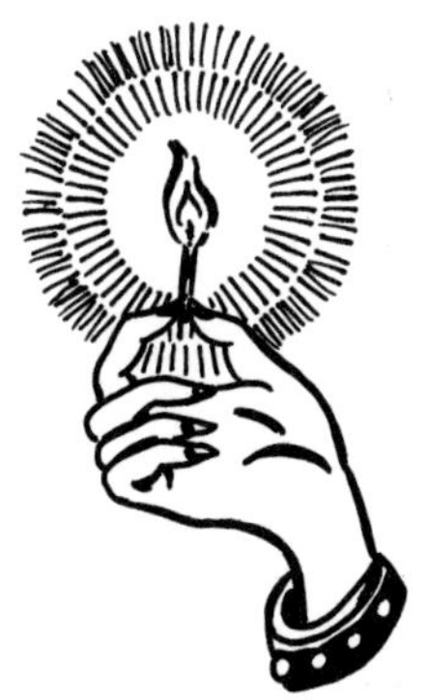

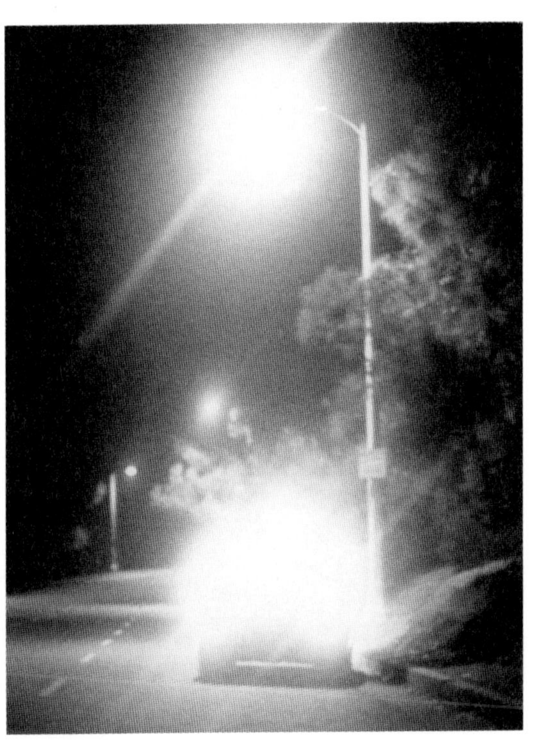

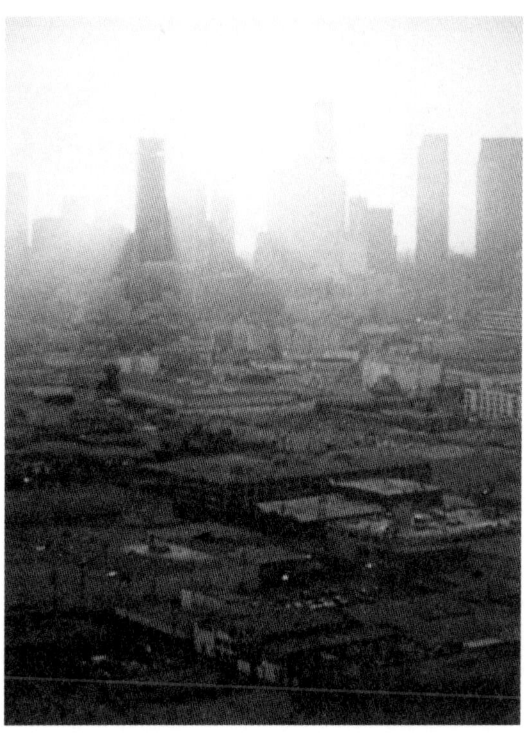

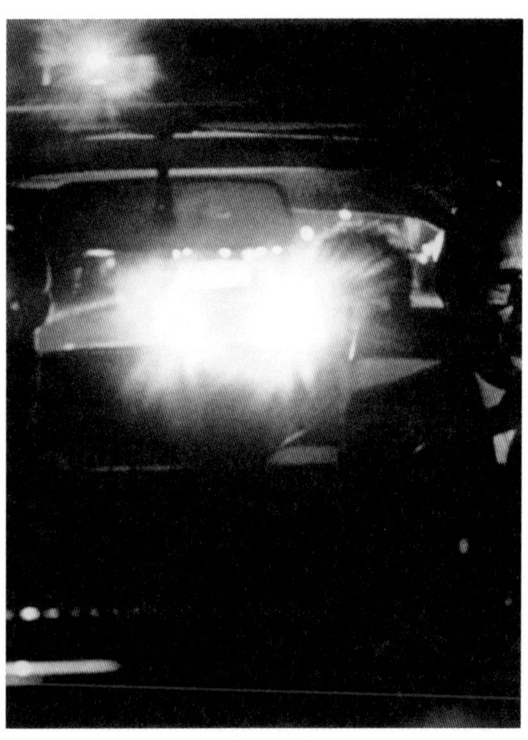

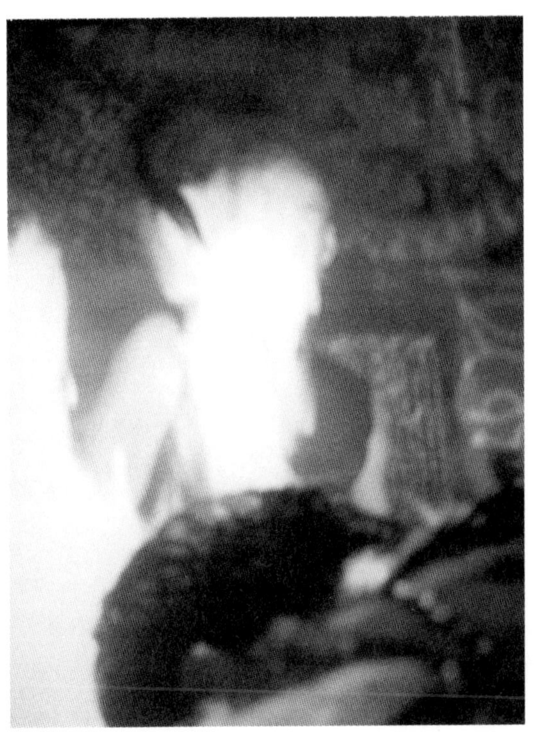

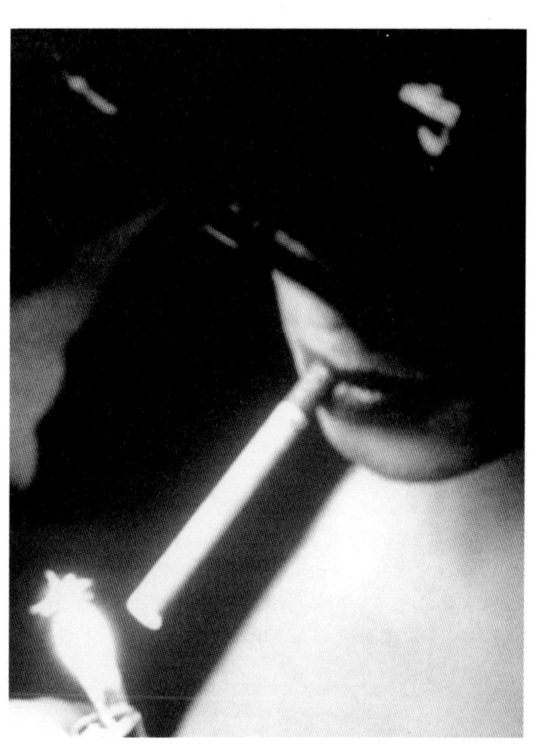

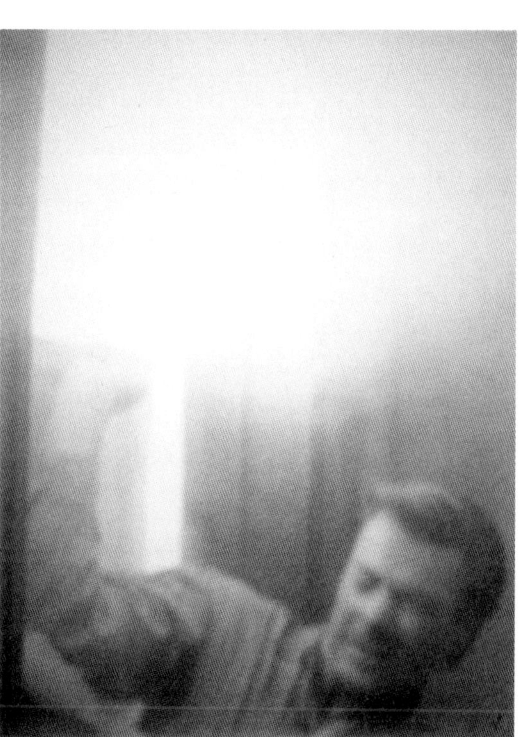

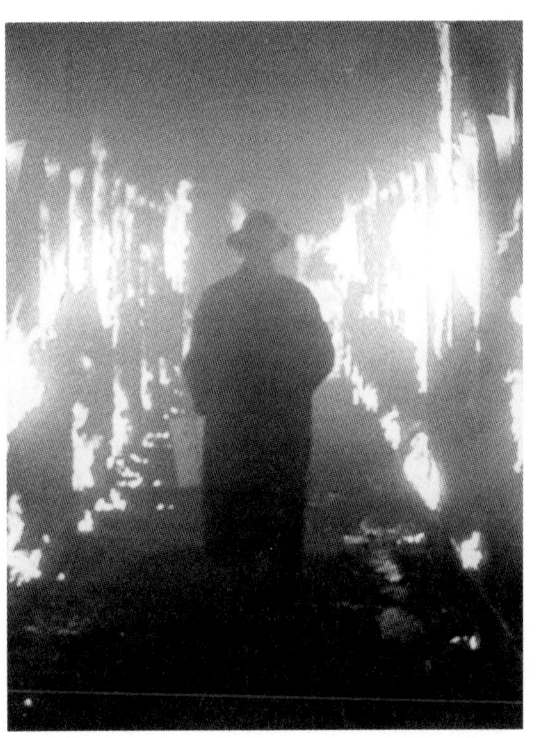

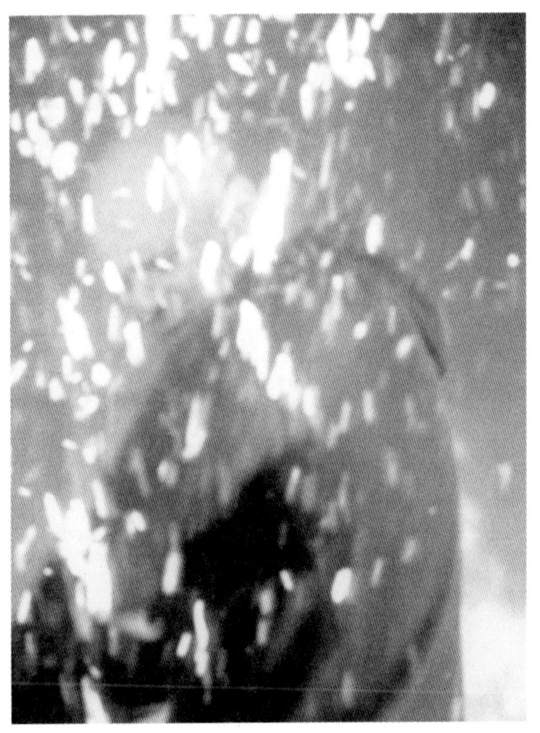

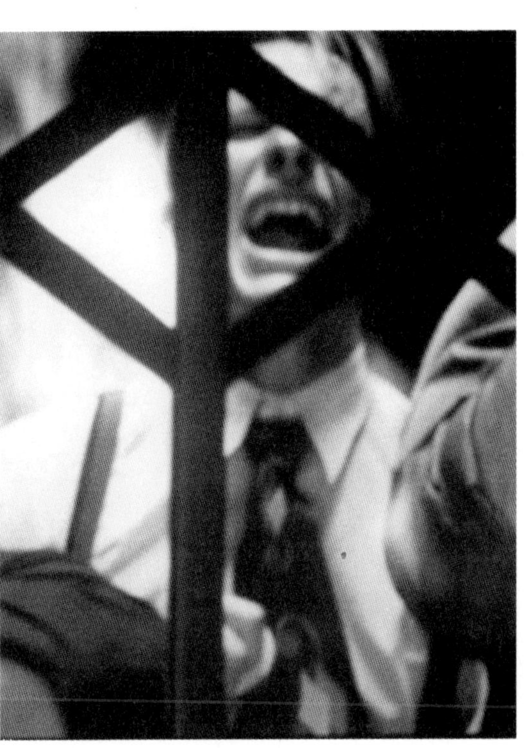

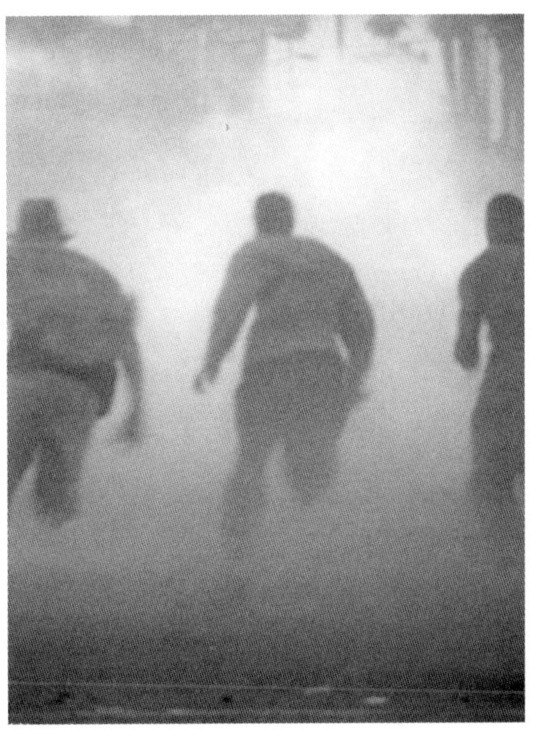

HONKY'S LADDER

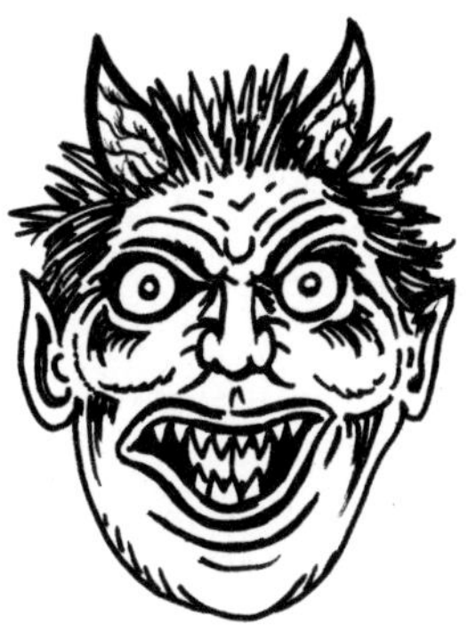

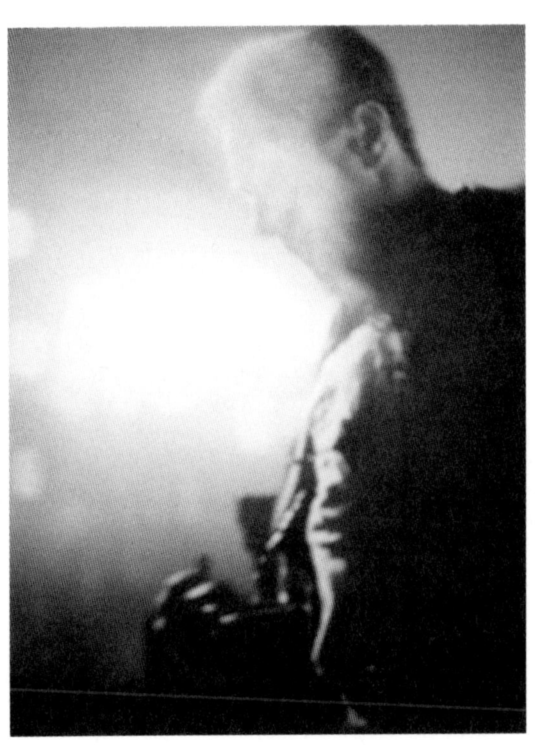

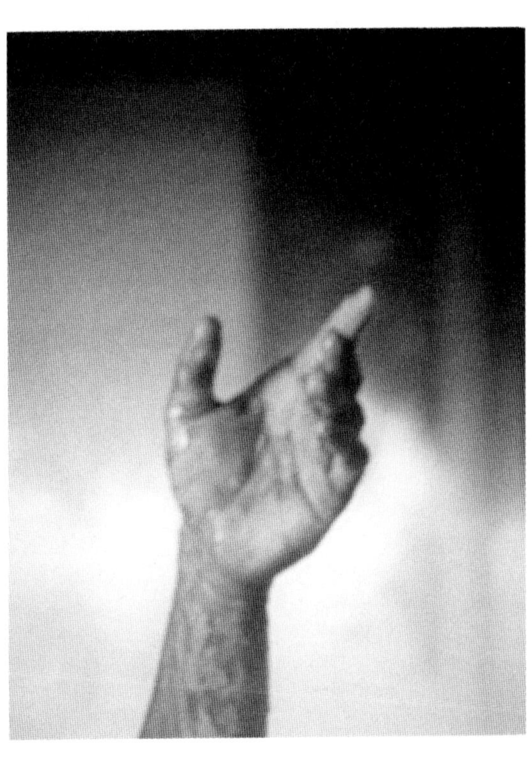

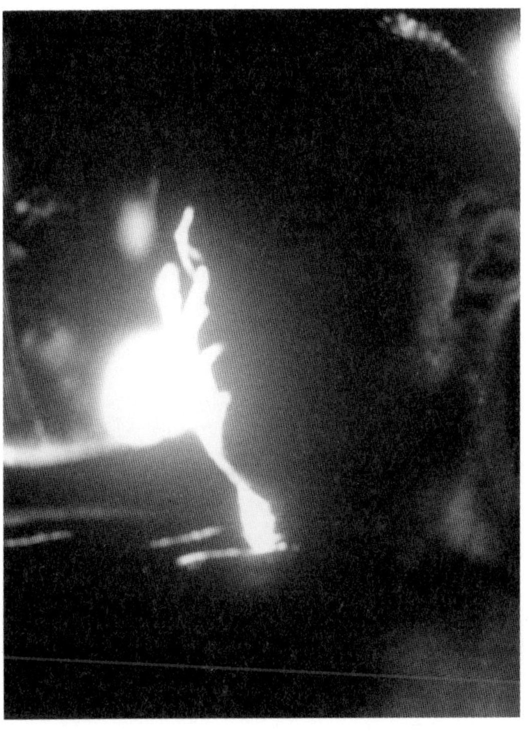

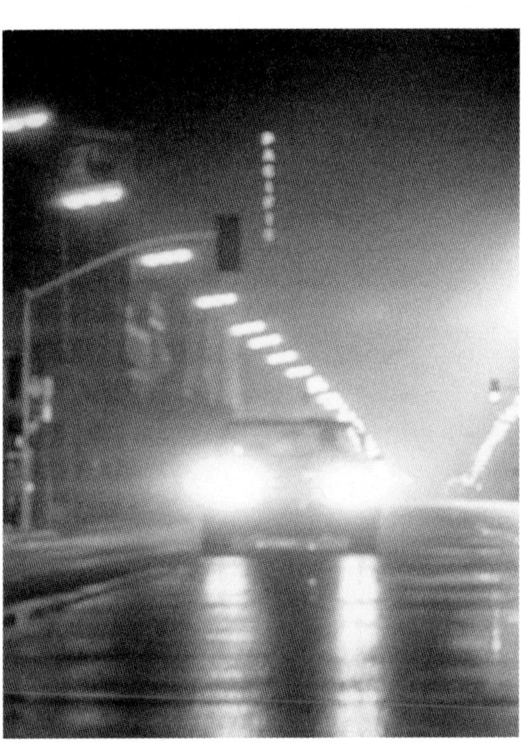

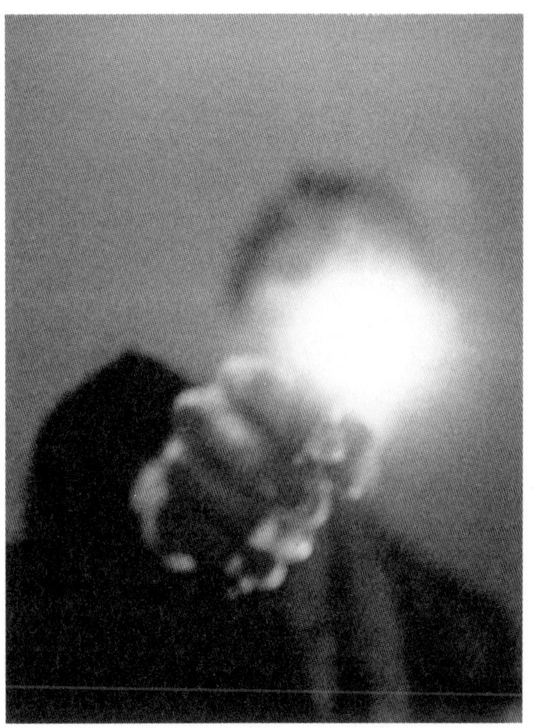

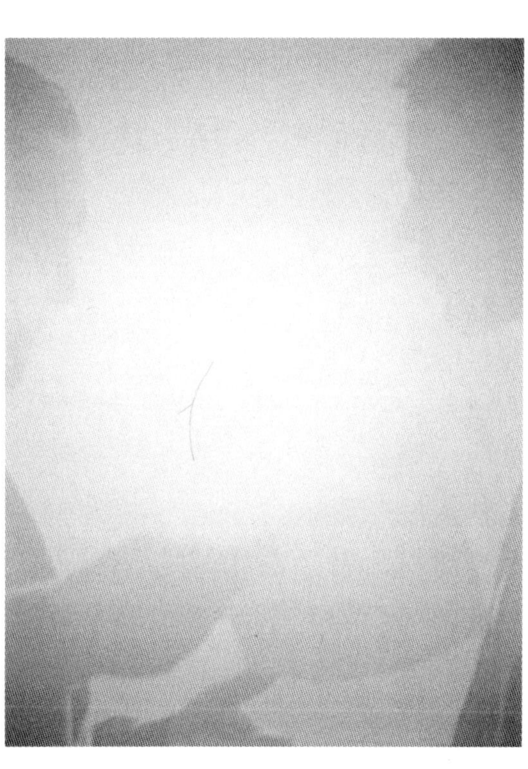

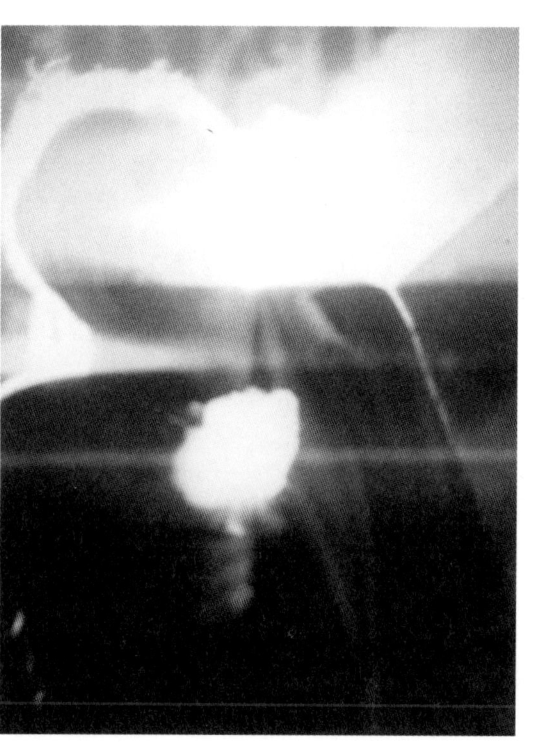

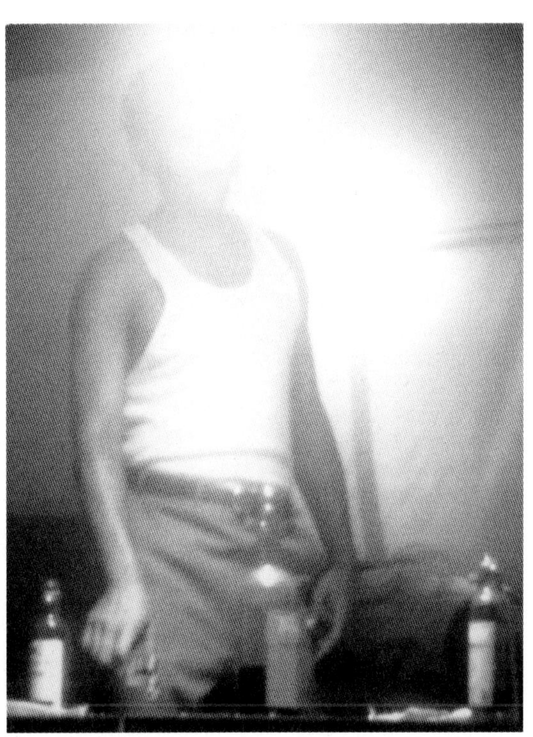

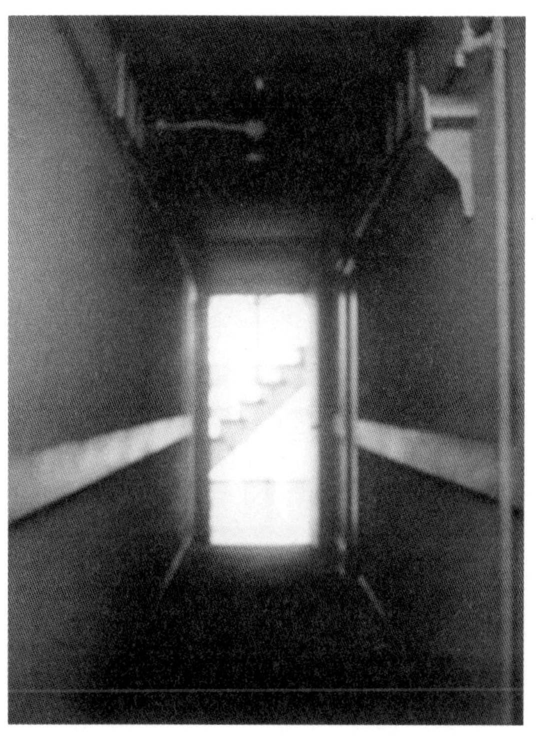

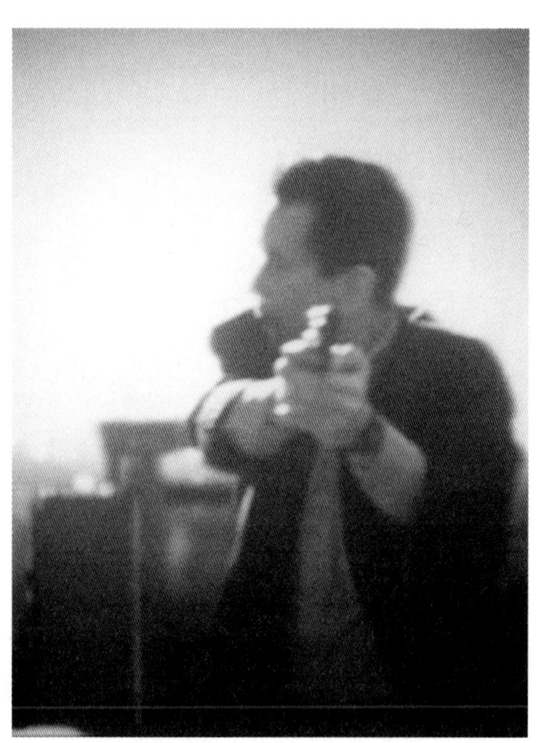

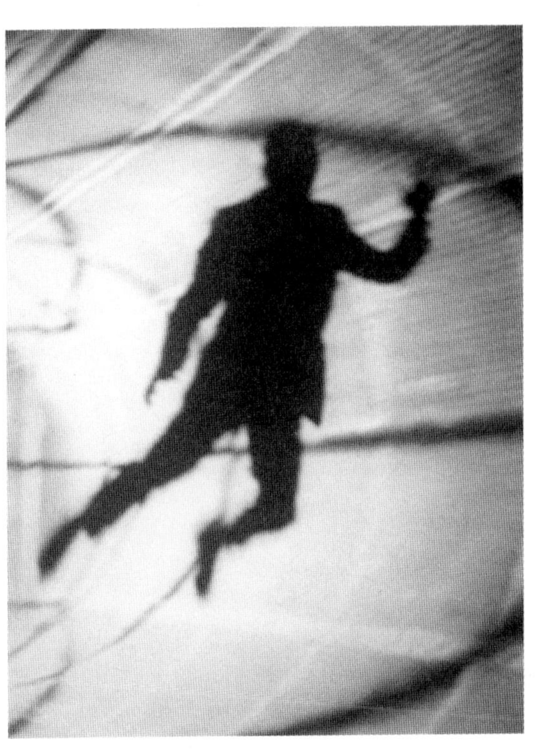

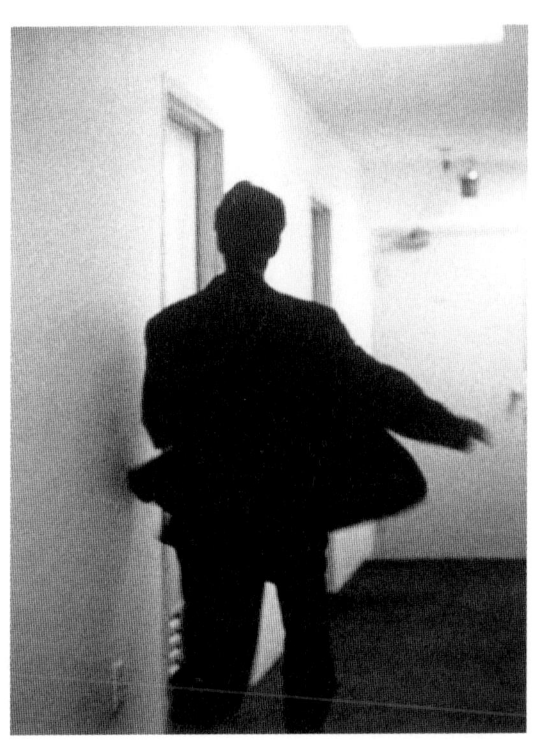

NIGHT BY CANDLELIGHT

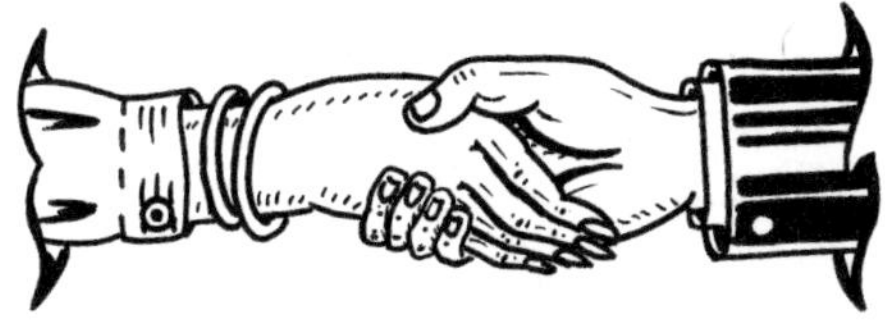

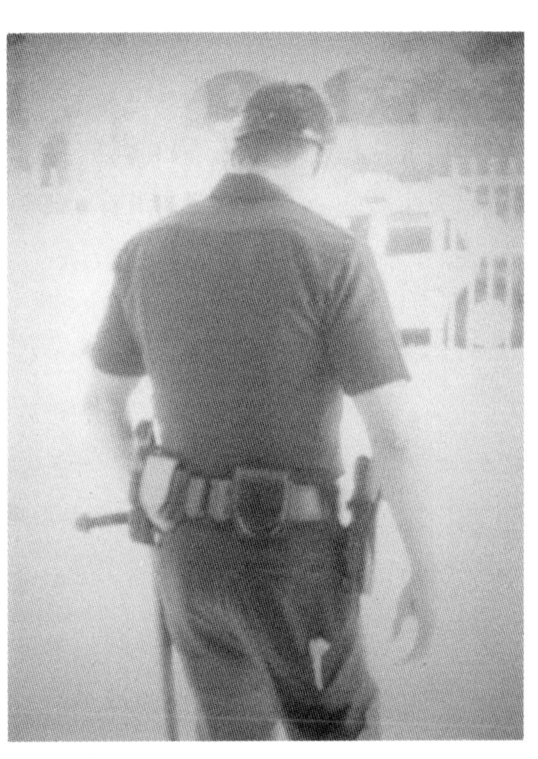

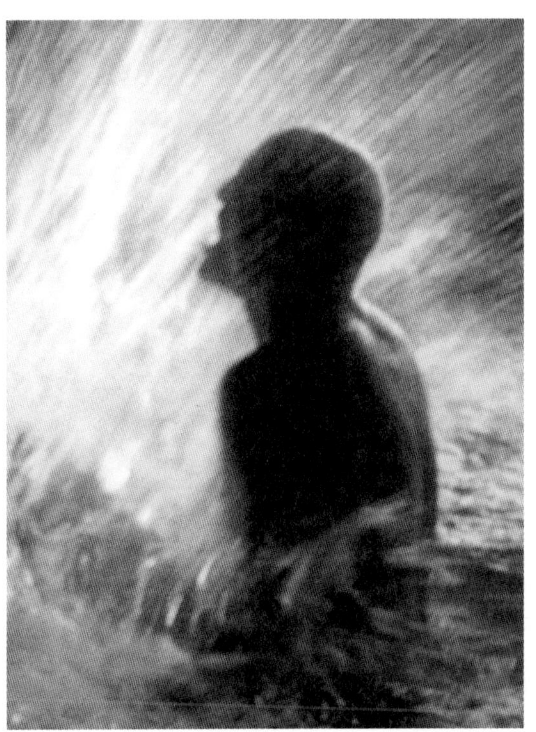

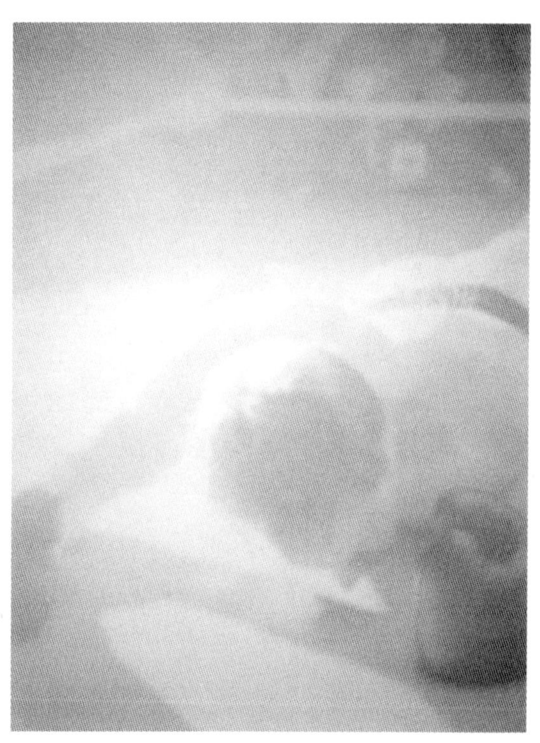

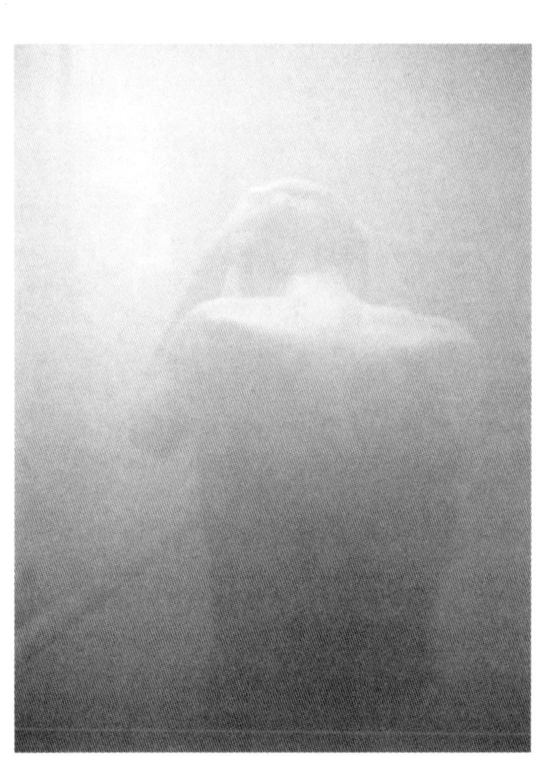

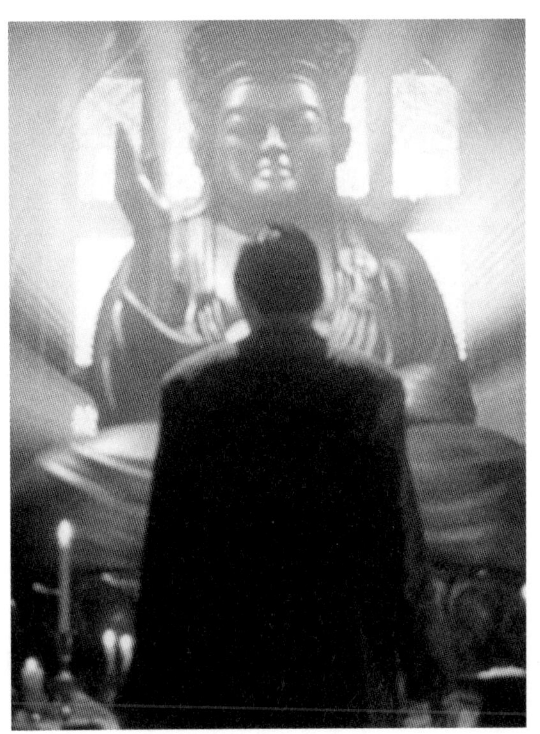

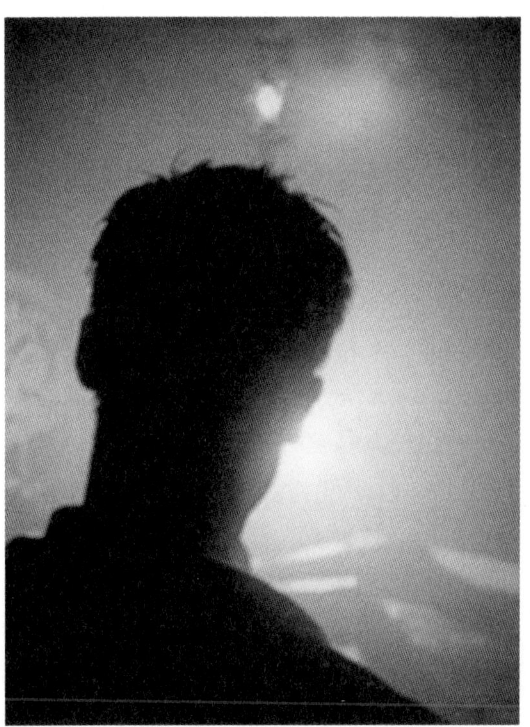

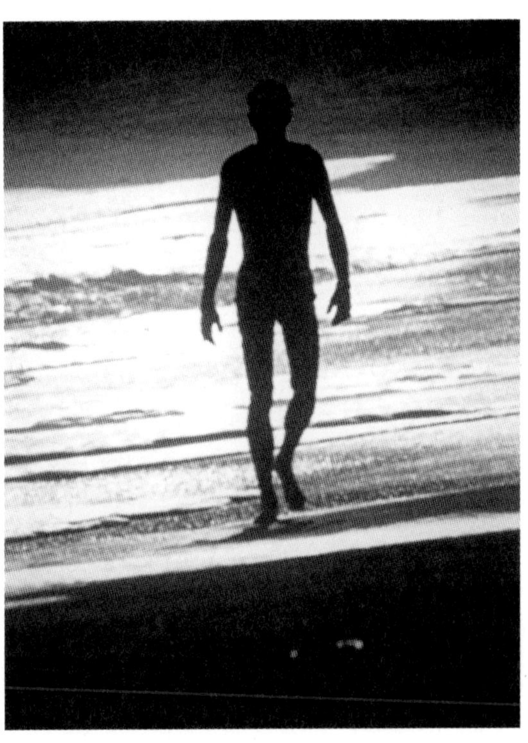

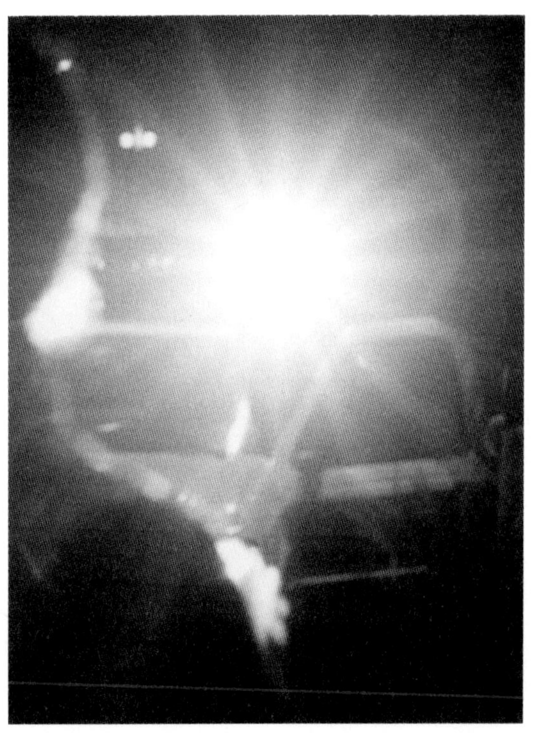

BULLETPROOF

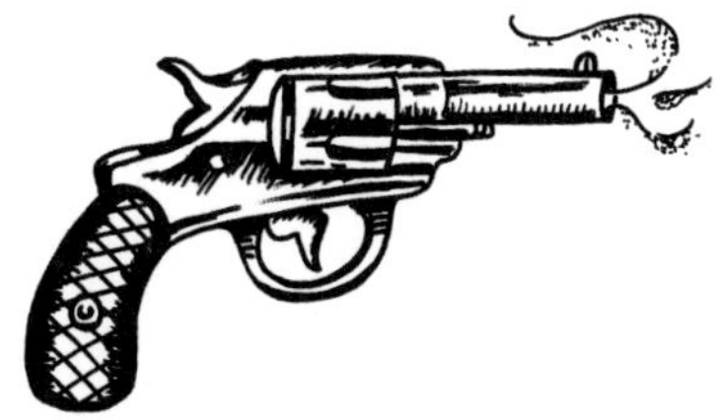

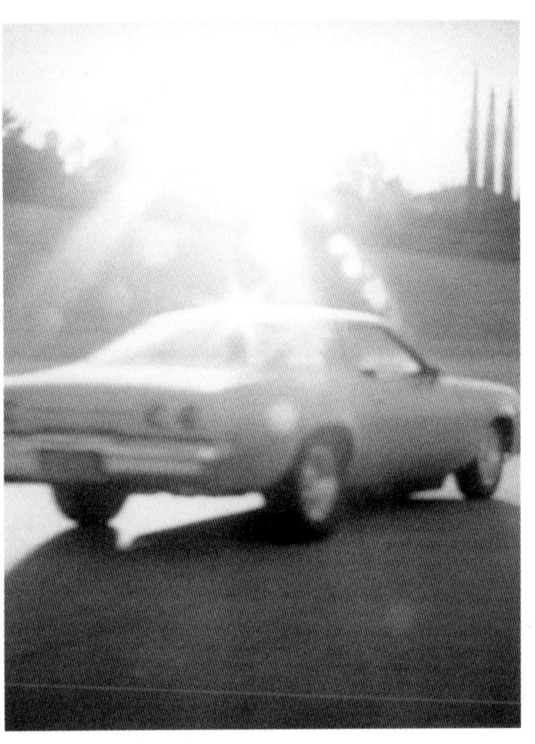

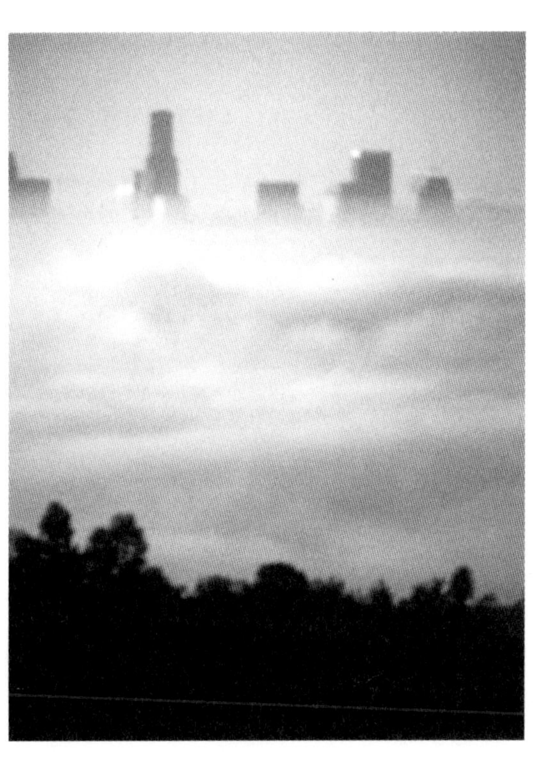

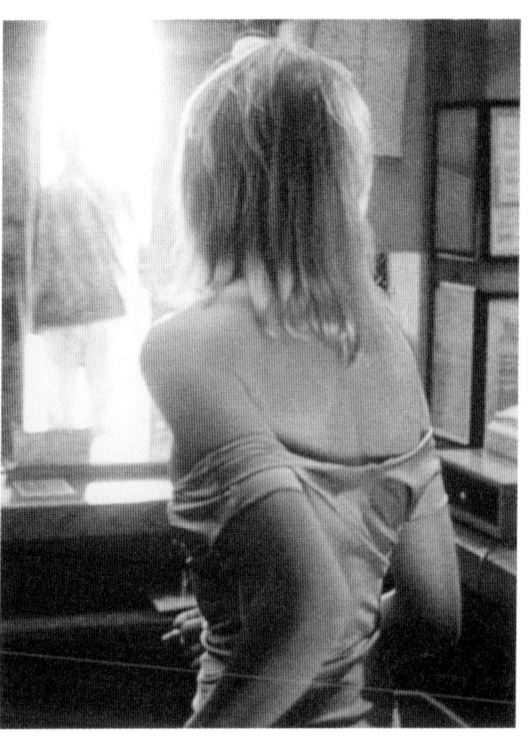

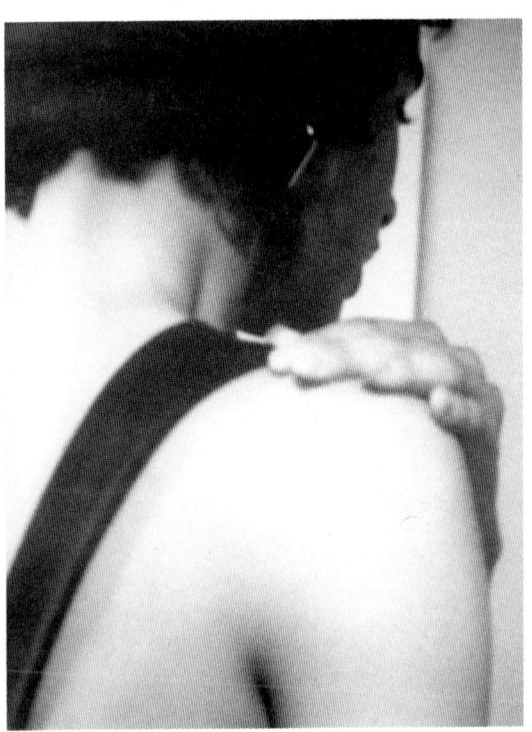

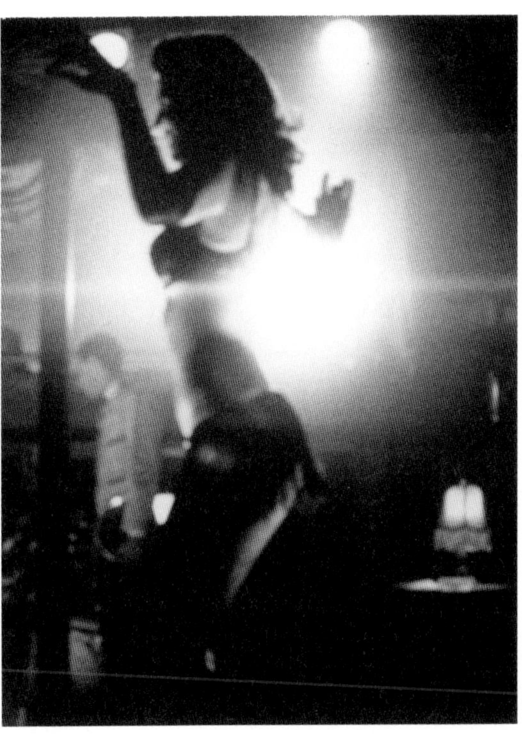

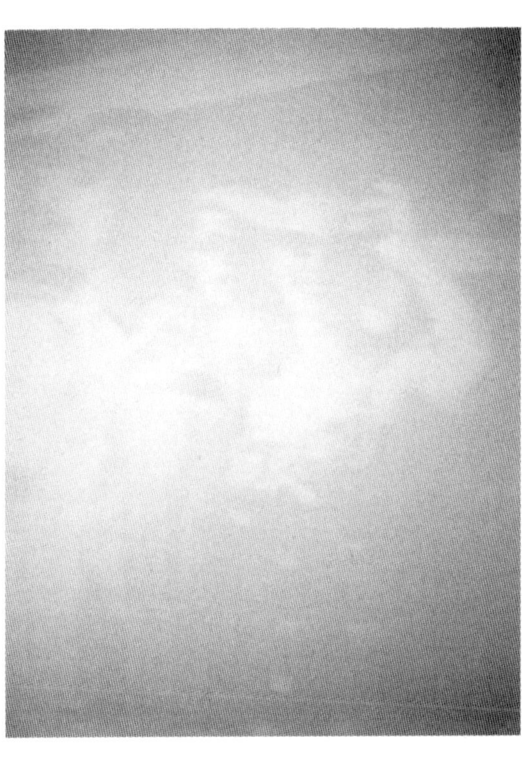

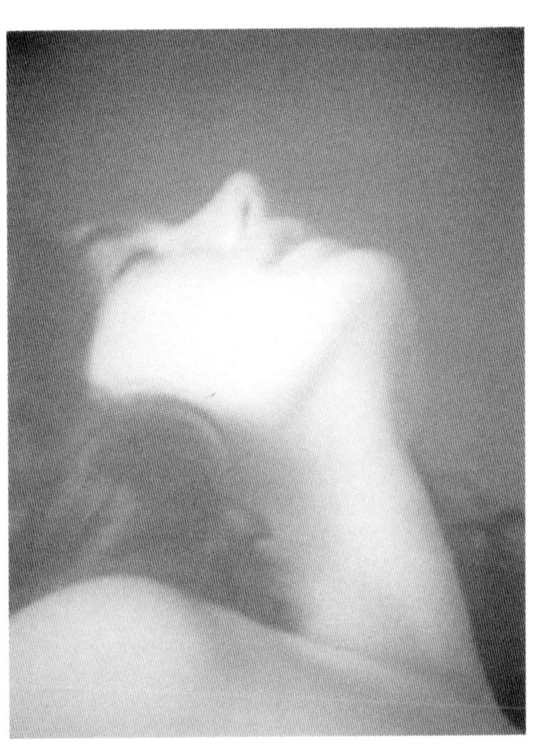

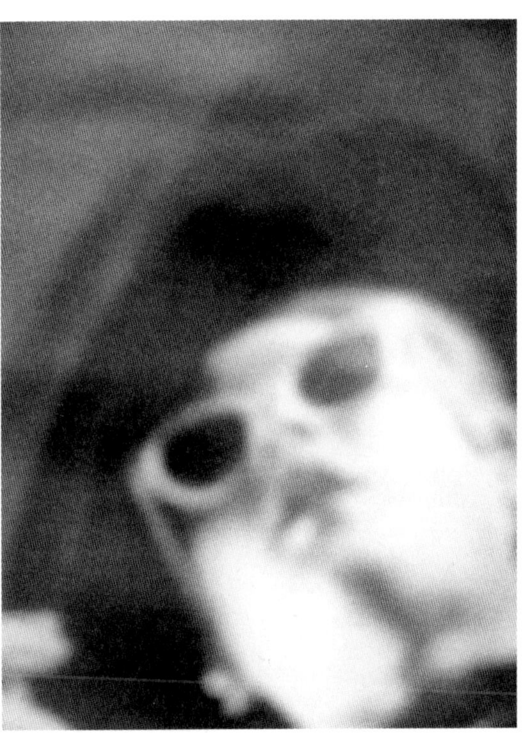

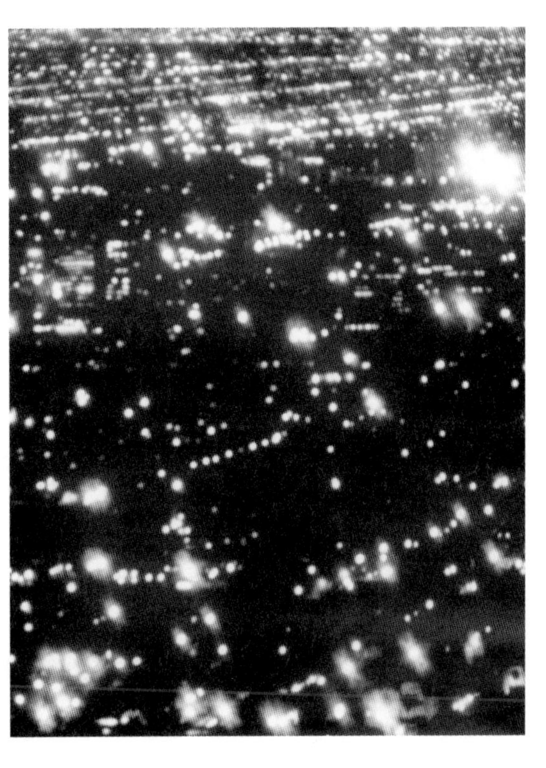

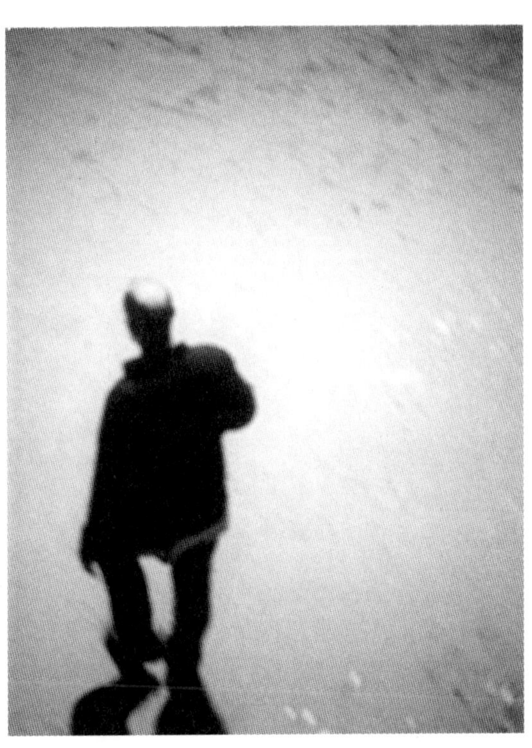

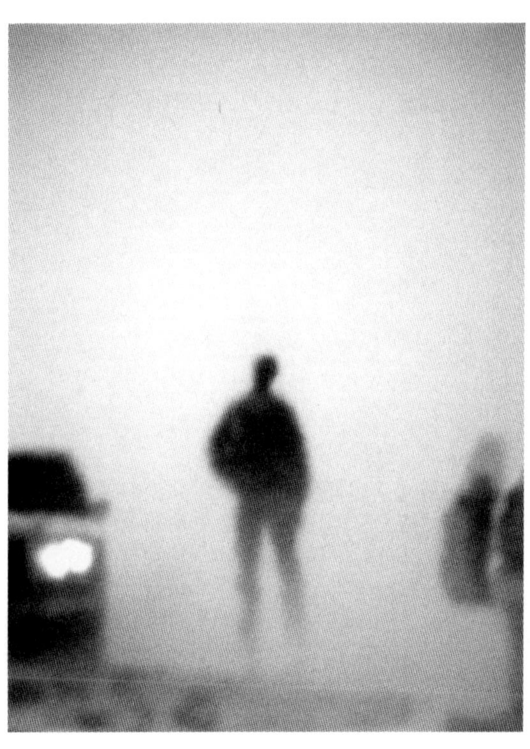

SUMMER'S KISS

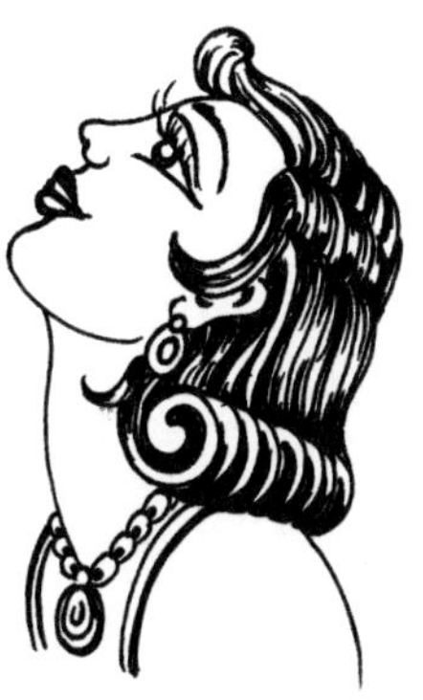

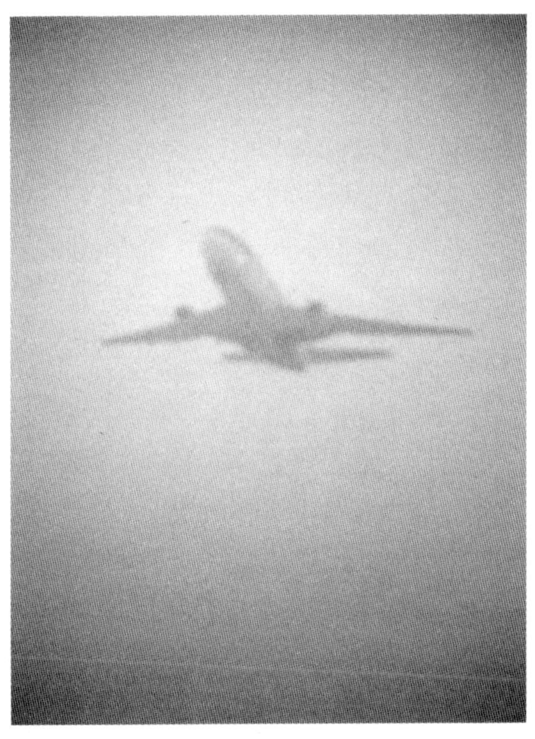

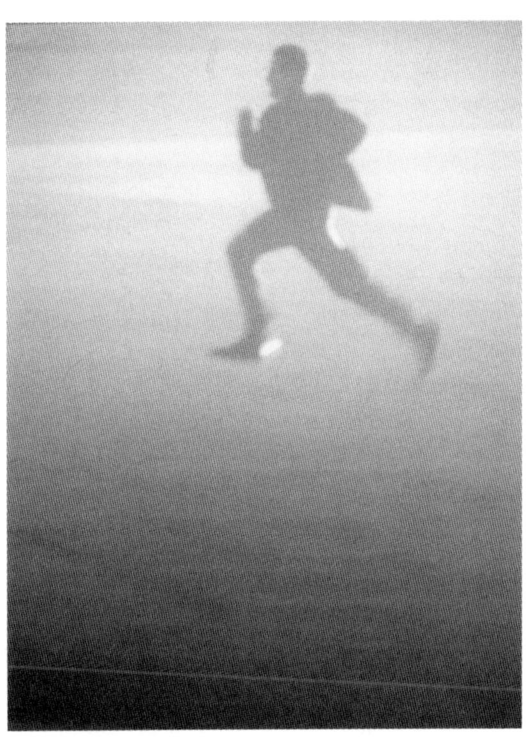

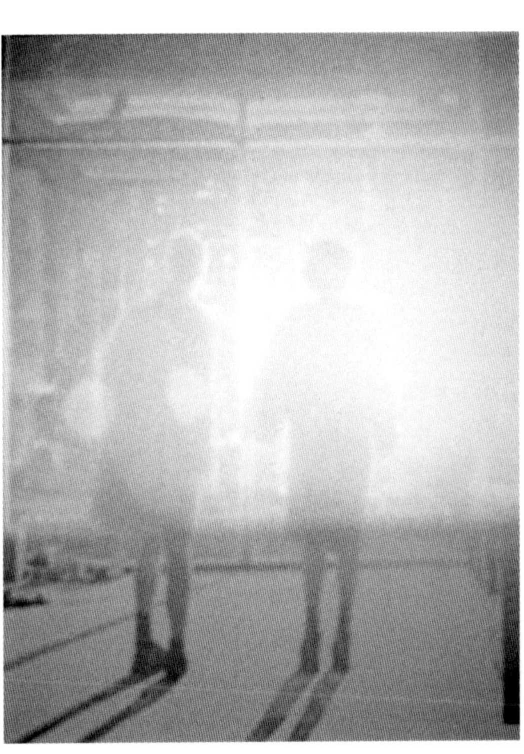

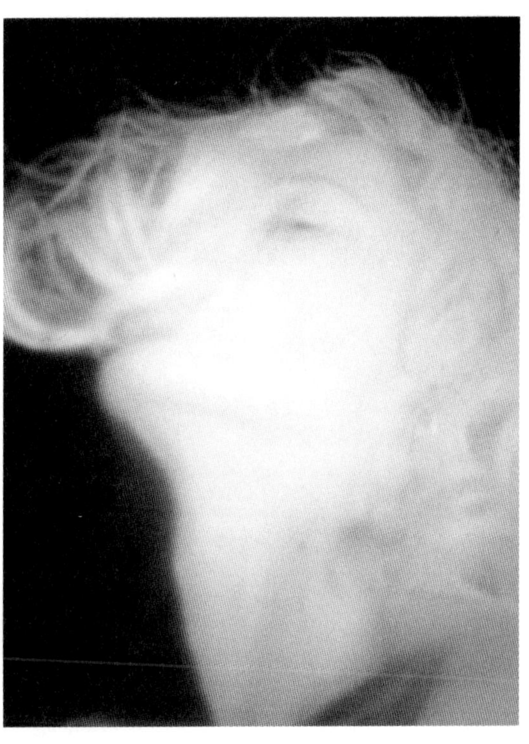

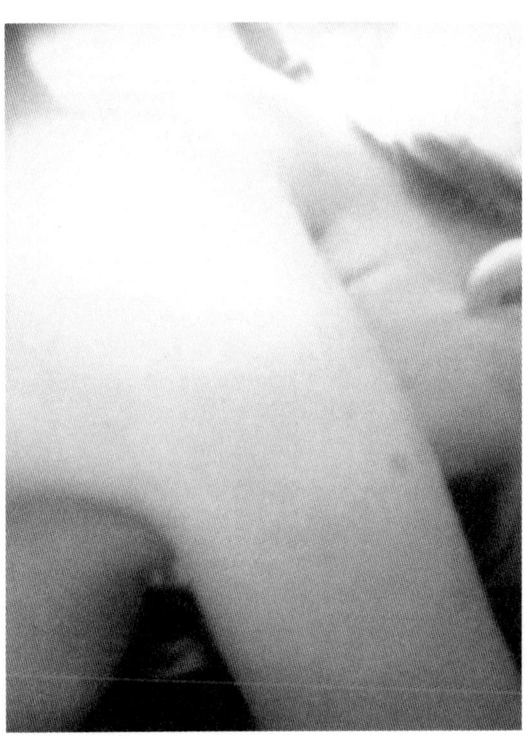

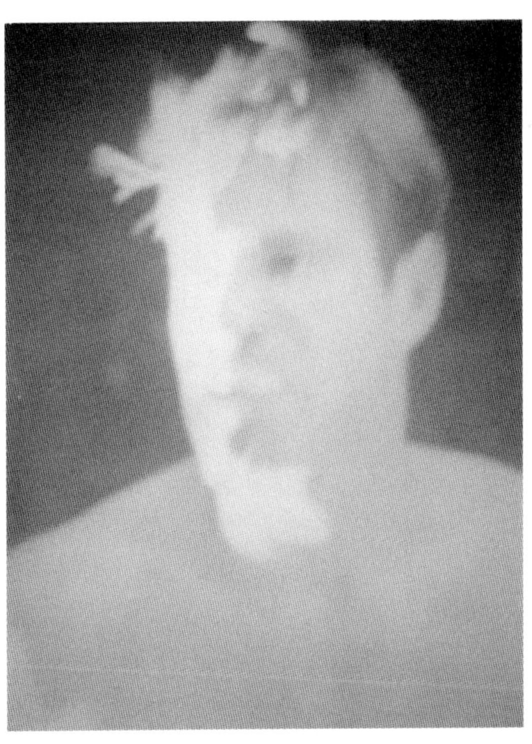

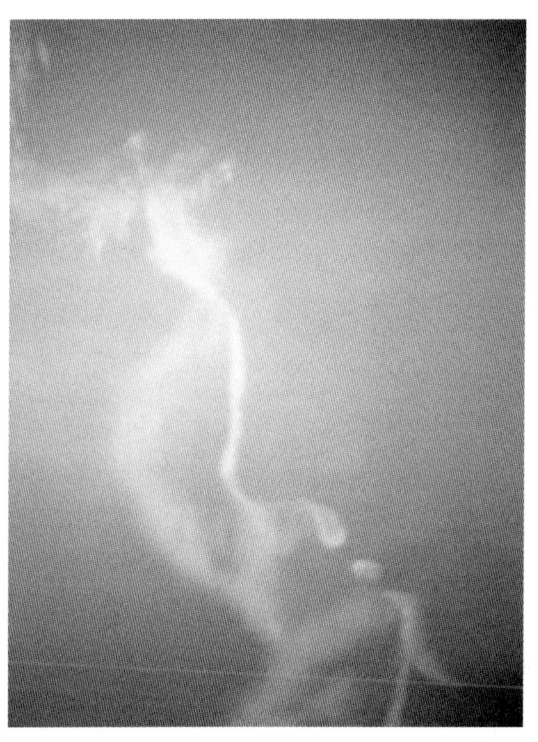

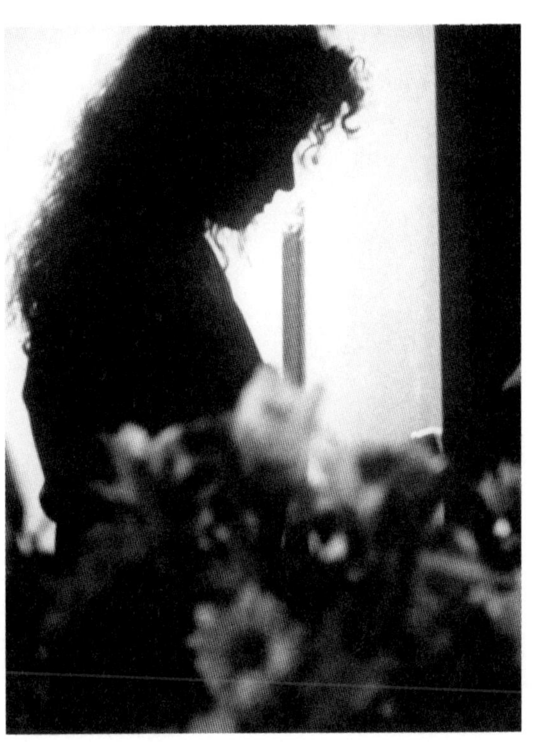

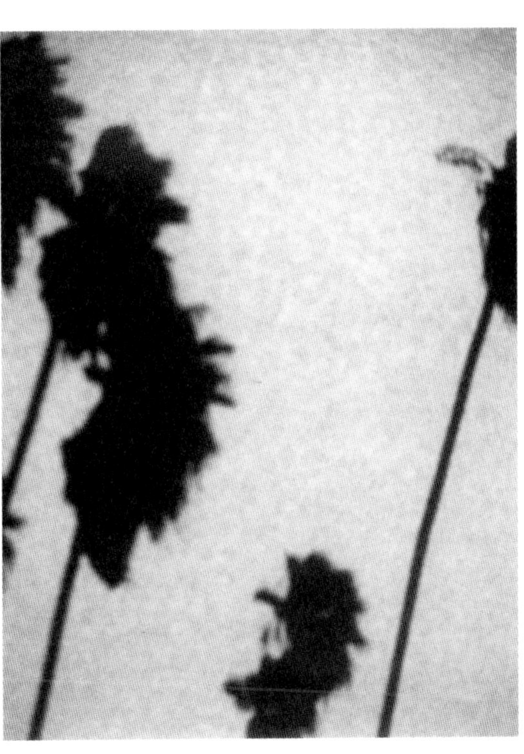

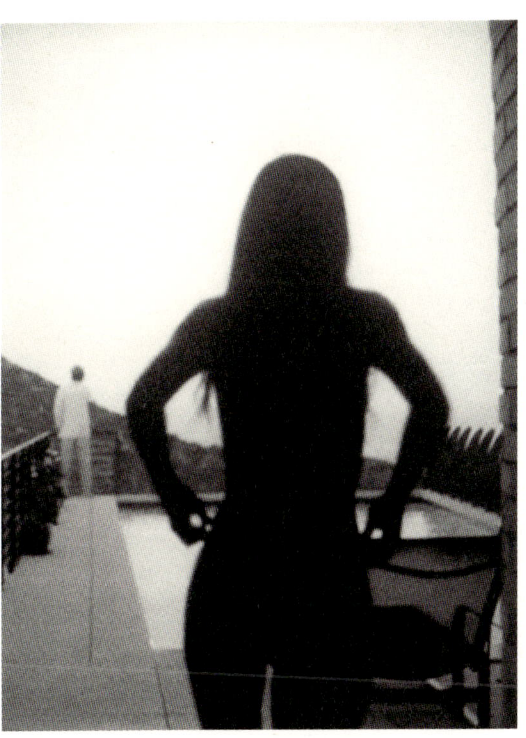

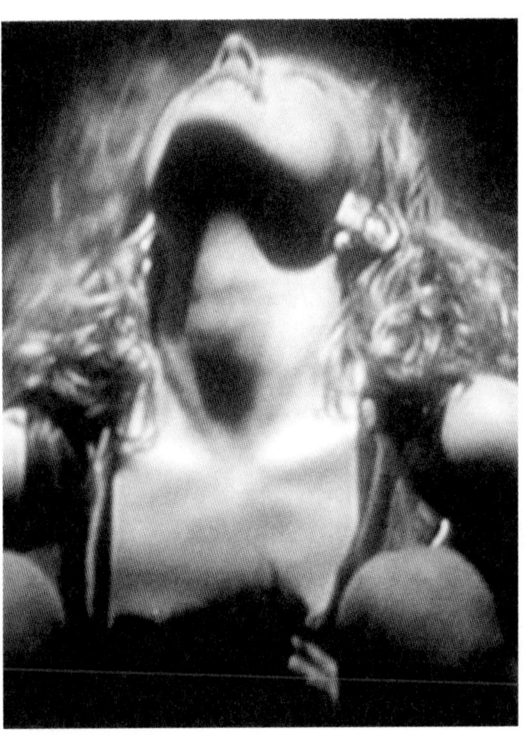

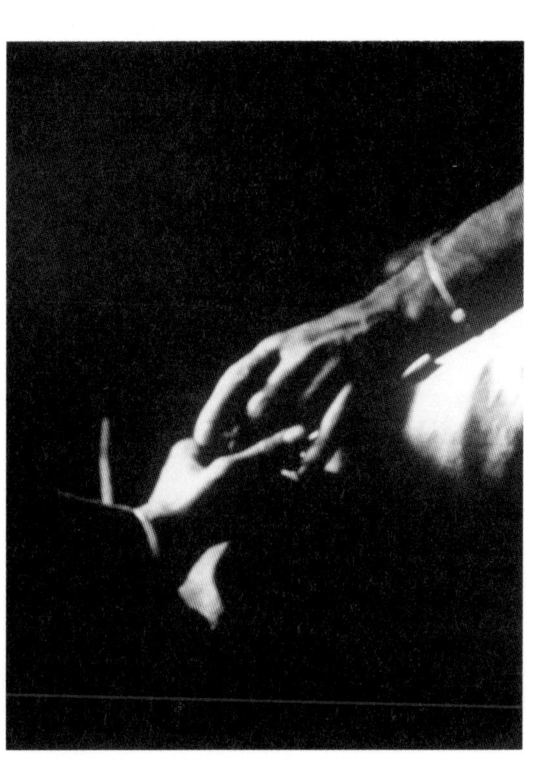

FADED

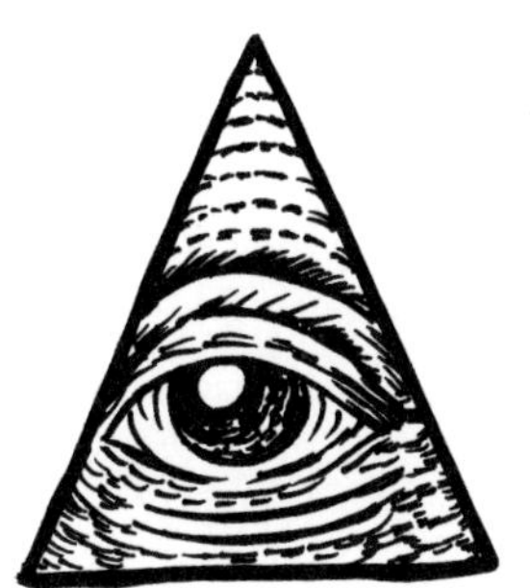

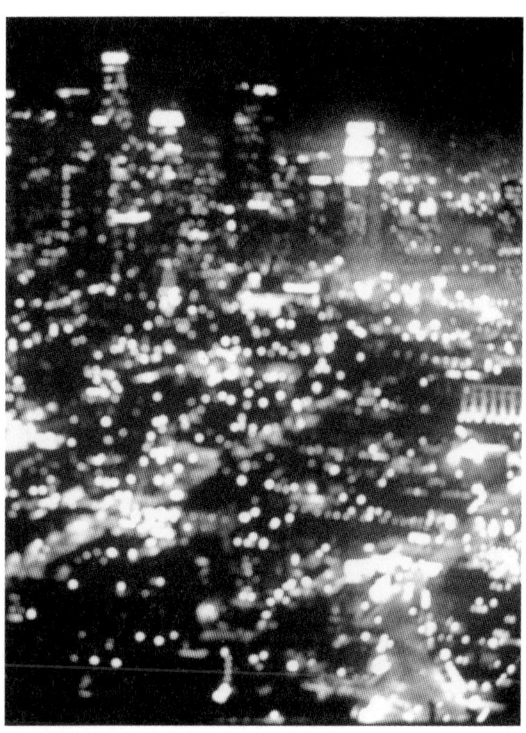

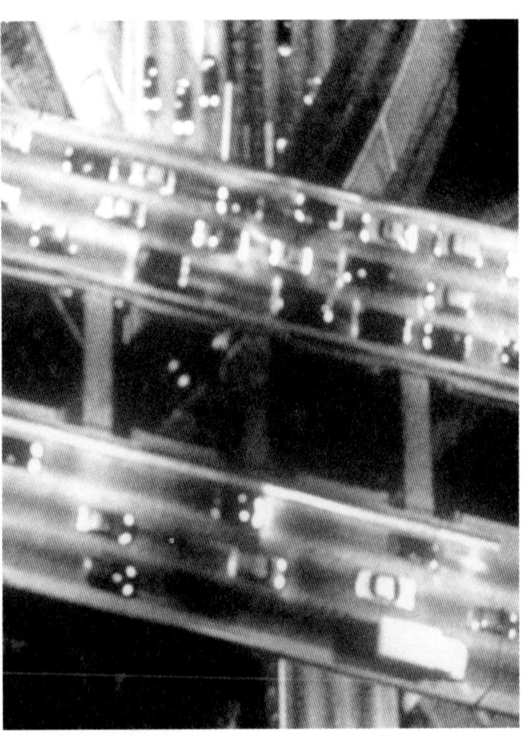

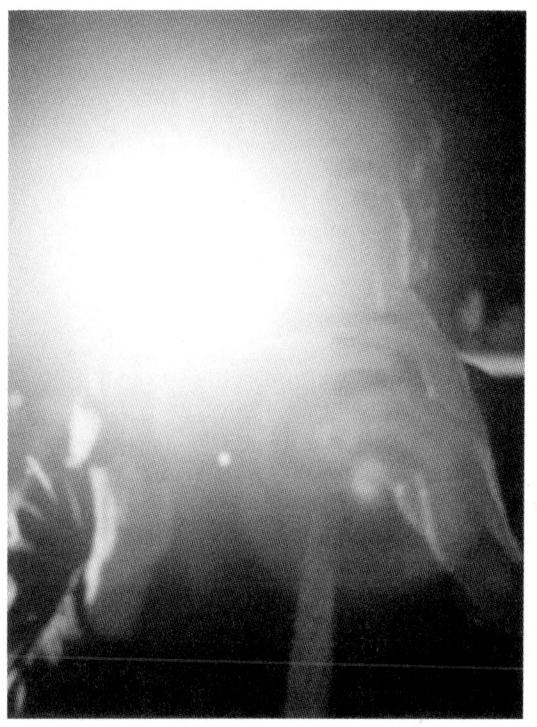

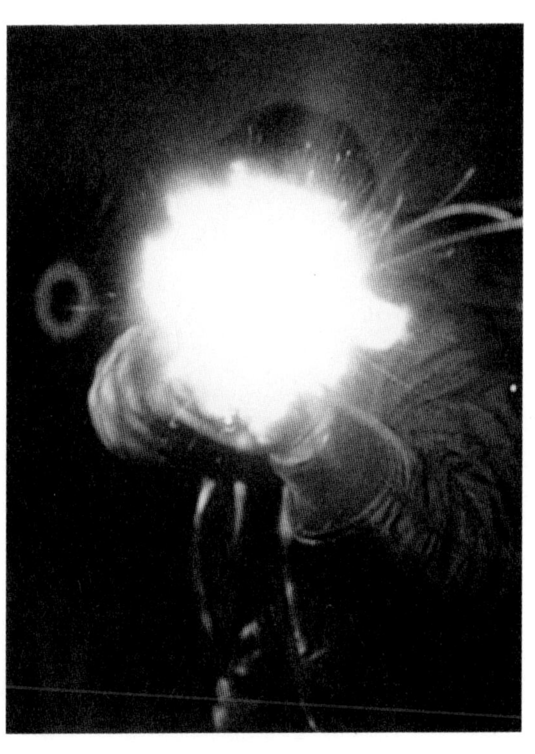

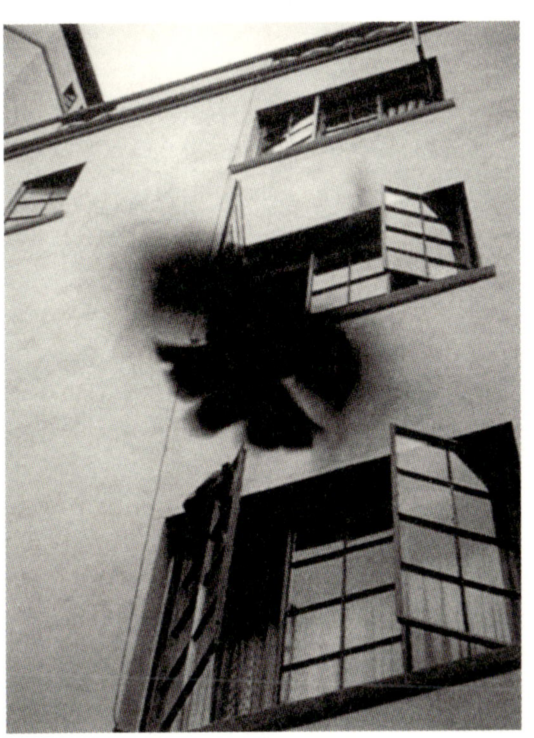

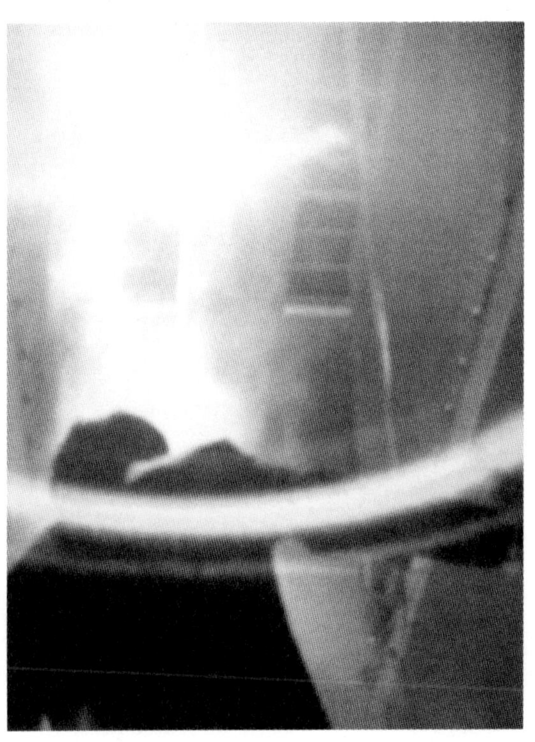

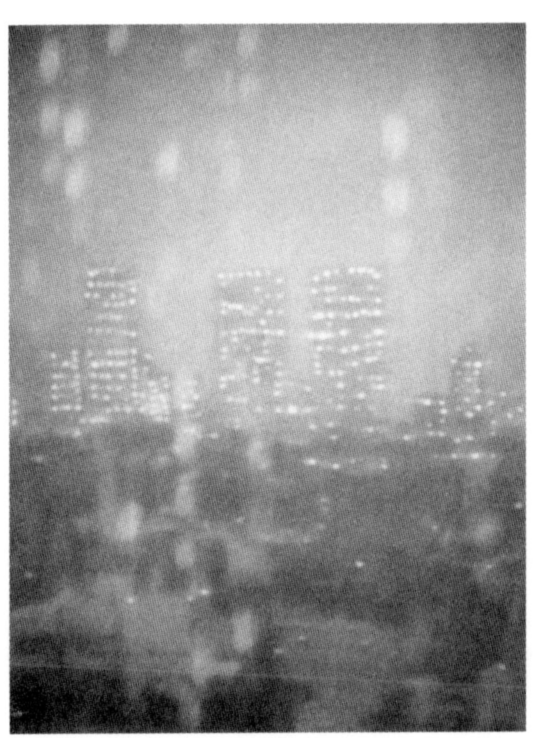

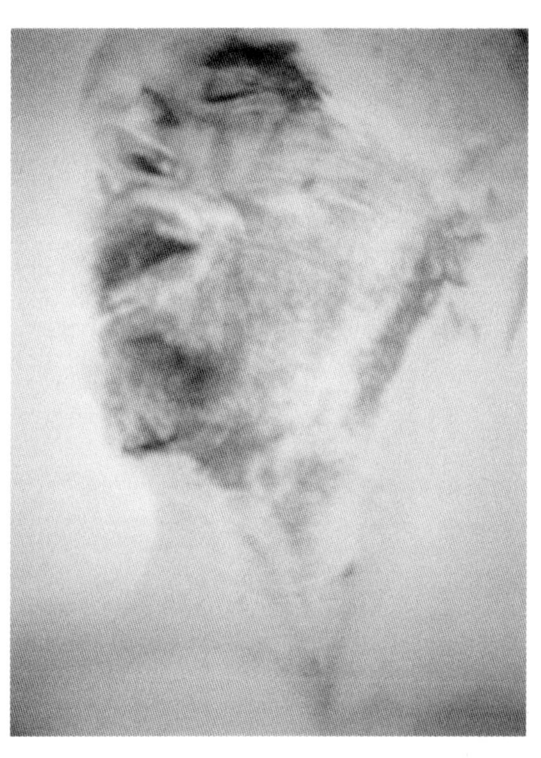

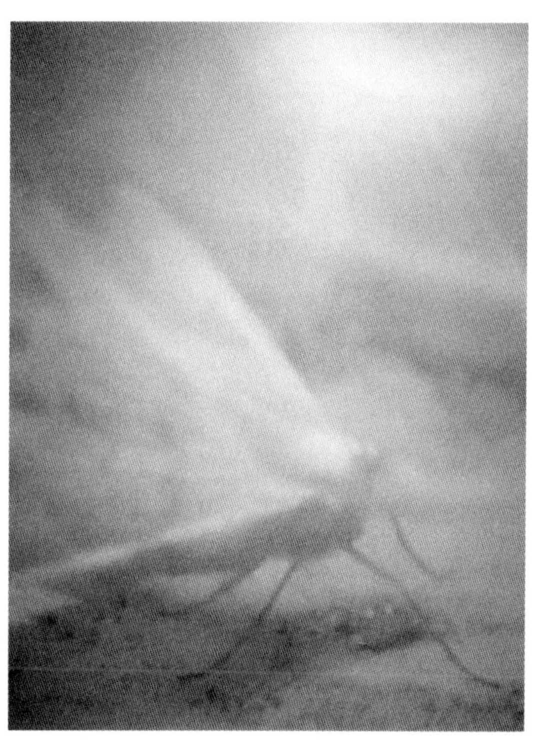

THE END.

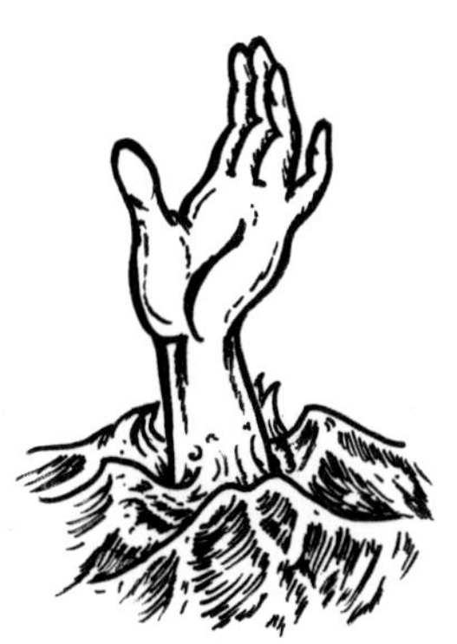

BLACK LOVE…

IN 1996 THE AFGHAN WHIGS released the album *Black Love.* As the legend goes, Greg Dulli, the lead singer and songwriter for the band, was inspired by Prince's Warner Bros. contract, which funded the film *Purple Rain*, and part of the Whigs' contract with Elektra stipulated that the label finance a feature-length film to be produced and directed by Dulli.

Time went by and the movie never surfaced. Rumor begat the legend that the album was in some way a soundtrack for the unrealized film. From this concept, the author of this book set out to visualize what that movie might have looked like. Inspired by neo-noir films, which roughly began with Robert Altman's *The Long Goodbye* (1973), he decided to set his version of the "film" in Los Angeles. After rephotographing excerpts from these films with a Polaroid Land Camera, he assembled them into a narrative that was analogous to the eleven-song cycle of *Black Love*, reverse engineering a storyboard for the movie that never was.

•••

THANK YOU...

THANK YOU TO *APERTURE*, who first published photos from this project in their summer 2018 issue, "Film & Foto."

Thank you to Rebecca Bengal for her haunting and visceral contribution to this project—the spiritual companion to these pictures that she conjured from the vapor of Los Angeles.

Thank you to Greg Dulli and The Afghan Whigs for *Black Love*, the album that inspired this cycle of photographs. Twenty-seven years after it was released, I still hear and feel something new every time the needle drops.

And thank you to Paul Schiek for his faith and enthusiasm in bringing this publication to life; his commitment to making some of my more ethereal ideas tangible; and his shared love for *Black Love*.

•••

CREDITS...

*There is no light at the end of the tunnel
because the tunnel is made of light*

© Edition...TBW Books, 2023
© Photographs...Ryan Spencer, 2023
© Illustrations...Chummy Alexanian, 2023
© Text..Rebecca Bengal, 2023

Interior design..Paul Schiek & Jason Munn
Cover design..Jason Munn
Project managers.......................................Joey Chipman & Claire Cichy
Illustrations...Chummy Alexanian

Be in touch...

Chummy: Tattoo 13 in Oakland, 510.655.1313
ryanspencerphoto.com
rebeccabengal.net
jasonmunn.com
tbwbooks.com

ISBN 978-1-942953-63-0
Printed in China